# Land of Dreams

John Irving Clarke

ISBN: 978-81-19654-28-4

First Edition: 2024
Rs. 200/-

Cyberwit.net
HIG 45 Kaushambi Kunj, Kalindipuram
Allahabad - 211011 (U.P.) India
http://www.cyberwit.net
Tel: +(91) 9415091004
E-mail: info@cyberwit.net



Printed at Repro India Limited.

*For* Julie,
the moon is climbing high…

# Contents

## Chapter One

# Cassandra Jackson

I love him to bits. Of course, I do. He's absolutely gorgeous. Sometimes when he's asleep I look at those lovely long eyelashes curling up and I watch his gentle breathing, the soft rise and fall of his chest, and my heart could burst with love.

Of course, I love him, I love him when he wakes and I hold him; we talk and we look out of the window down on to the tiny figures scurrying below, the little old ladies clutching their shopping bags and leaning into the wind; the traffic bustling along the main road. I'll point out all of the kids as they leave school and anything else of excitement we can see: stray dogs sniffing the playground swings, birds being hurled across the sky or any break in the unrelenting grey. Best of all, even though he'll never see us from down there, we look to see Daddy coming home for his tea and we'll wave and point. Both of us: me and Will. I love him, of course I love him, I think of him first thing in the morning and last thing at night, but I also know he drains all of my energy, he sucks me dry.

I decided to call him Will. There are no Wills, Williams or Bills in our family, or at least I don't think there are, I called him Will after a lad I used to know; a nice lad who was ever so polite and he always tried to do the right thing. You can't knock anyone for that, can you? No, I used to like Will even though he'd annoy the hell out of me sometimes. I haven't seen him for ages and the truth be told, I don't want to see him again either. All of that was a long time ago, and it's not a place I really want to revisit.

No, Will and I are fine. Will and me. Me and Will. Me and Will and his daddy: Simon, of course. We're all fine and I'd much rather look to the future than the past, that's for sure. There's a lot of nasty stuff in the past and I'm better off trying to forget about it all.

It's easier said than done. How did I ever get into this position: sitting looking down on the world from my sixth floor flat like a Queen surveying her lands, or in my more desperate moments, Rapunzel waiting for her saviour prince? Cassandra Jackson: Cassie, one-time daydreamer and mother of the adorable Will. Okay, he's adorable, but don't let's pretend that he doesn't make an ear-piercing racket sometimes. He's adorable when he's asleep, but when he's awake he's a source of constant demands: feed me, change me and entertain me. And I do all of those things because I love him, I do all of those things and it leaves me shattered.

Sometimes I count the minutes until Simon comes home. I check the clock and then later I'll check it again and I could swear it hasn't moved. I feel like shaking it really hard to see if it is still working. I'd throw it across the room if I thought that would help. And when Simon does come home, does he want to hear all about my day of feeding, changing and playing with the baby? Well what do you think?

I do my best. I always try to make the flat look reasonably ship-shape. I give my hair a brush and I have the tea pot full and ready to give him a nice welcome home because this *is* Simon's home now. I couldn't bear to have him think any other way. He's earning and he's done well. He'll be taken on permanently by his firm soon and that'll mean an increase in money. I know lots of lads Simon's age would prefer to spend their money with their mates, having a beer and a laugh, chasing other girls, and there's plenty who would have him, where do you think Will gets his looks from? But no, Simon comes home here, to Will and to me, the mother of his child.

We do okay. We don't get out much unless you count the weekends when we load up the buggy and, if the lifts aren't working, we climb down the endless flights of cold, concrete stairs and we set out to walk through the park, go and see the ducks perhaps. Weather permitting, we'll stop on a bench for a cup of tea each, and sometimes, if a devil-may-care mood takes us, we'll also have a biscuit or a piece of cake.

We used to go by the football pitches but not anymore. We caught the end of a match once as the Pink Ladies F.C., the team I used to play for, came trooping off the pitch with mud on their knees and victory in their smiles. The girls flocked around and they had Will out of his buggy in no time fussing over him and making baby noises, "Googoo googoo goo. You're lovely you are!" and saying how lucky I was. But I saw the looks on their faces, they could go and get showered and plan a boisterous night of booze and boys. They didn't ask if I wanted to come along or if I was going to start playing again, they didn't need to. Simon and I headed back to the six flights of stairs and our tiny flat. No, as I say, we don't go round that way now.

So how do we manage? Not too badly actually. Simon earns a bit and most months we usually make ends meet. Luckily, Dad often pushes some money our way. He says he's doing well. He always did like to talk up his dreams and achievements and he hasn't changed at all. So, he gives us money for his first grandchild, and I take it because it might just ease his conscience as well.

Mum's great considering what she's fighting against. It was a bit strained at first as I thought we could all move in with her: me, Simon and the baby. After all, there was plenty of room, but she more or less threw me out. She knew what she was doing when she said it was no place to start off together. Now she'll often pop round when her shift allows and she loves to sit on the rug with Will but she'll also roll up her sleeves and get cracking with the hoover or a duster. "You know me and dusty houses," she says.

She and Simon get on well together too, which is just as well as Simon's lot don't really bother with us. We did try for a while, taking Will round in the buggy; you'd have thought they were pleased to see us, or at least pleased to see Simon and Will, maybe not me: the evil witch Cassandra who had cast her spell. No, the atmosphere was vile.

The clink of a spoon on a saucer could reverberate for hours and there was nothing else to crack the ice of silence. Simon's dad, I always had a soft spot for him, he said once as he saw us out of the front garden gate, "Don't worry. Give it time and people will come round." Okay, so now we are giving it time.

Did I mention Alison, Simon's sister? Ali and I are best mates. Or at least we used to be but not anymore. What the hell happened? I try to piece it all together sometimes, how we used to work together at school; she was brilliant, we played football, messed about in each other's bedroom and talked about all kinds of things. But there was also jealousy, mine I suppose, and that business about me changing schools. There's the other stuff too: my stupid daydreams, my drifting around the past and the present. It got to the stage where I didn't know where the hell I was, so how could anyone else keep track of me? Plus, she'll never forgive me for ruining Simon's life.

All I know is that I used to be a good girl once. Here's a word for you: schizophrenia, go and look that up. I did, it means a mental illness, gradually losing your mind or your personality to enter into another reality. Doesn't sound good does it? Is that me? A schizophrenic? I don't think so; I just think I allowed imagination to overact, looking for a better world than reality. It was hardly a better world though, it was awful. It was like a giant trapdoor which I've slammed shut and I daren't let it open again. I know it's still there though; I've just got to guard against letting it creak open just the slightest.

So how do I make sense of it all now? How do I piece this jigsaw together? It's a mess, a complete mess, but like every jigsaw you should start with the corners. So that would be friendship in one corner, rivalry, competition and jealousy in another and then daydreams could definitely go in a third. So that leaves the fourth corner for the biggest, ugliest piece of the jigsaw, the bit which casts a dark shadow over the rest refusing to fit in easily anywhere. It's the bit of the jigsaw where even just thinking about it now makes me want to throw up.

## Chapter Two

# Alison Jones

No, I don't want to speak about Cassie Jackson. Why should I? We were mates, best mates, and now we're not; simple as that.

Angry? Of course I am, and sometimes I'm a little bit sad, but that just makes me feel angrier. We would do almost everything together: we worked together at school, we played football together and we were always around at each other's houses. So where did it all go wrong? Was it when she just suddenly upped sticks and moved to a new school for her GCSEs? I've no idea.

I know I used to get fed up with her fantasies. I mean we all like to drift off occasionally, but she would take it too far. She'd enter a completely different world and talk to me about things and I would have no idea what she was carrying on about. Where did she get to? I sometimes used to wonder if she was on something. You know, taking something. There was definitely something which was having a bad effect on her. Maybe her dad being away from home bothered her. I don't know; she was sometimes upset when he wasn't there, but to be honest, she was often upset when he was.

I suppose there were times when I could have been a better friend. Sometimes I lost patience with her when she got so wrapped up in some thing she wouldn't tell me about. I didn't realise it at the time, but the laughs began to dry up and there was usually something niggling away at her; if only she'd told me about it, whatever it was. We used to do a lot of work together at school but then she'd like to take all of the credit, like she had to be the best at everything. What did she have to prove? That wasn't nice, that wasn't nice at all.

Not nice? O yes, don't believe what you might have heard about Cassie Jackson being all sweet and innocent; Cassie Jackson and truth are often complete strangers. Don't take pity on those big, doleful eyes. She knows how to use those eyes, *and* everything else. She took in my brother completely: hook, line and sinker. Simon could have been anything he wanted; he could have had the pick of all the top universities. Now he's doing a crap job and he's holed up in that tower block flat knee deep in soiled nappies. Whose fault is that?

I said I didn't want to speak about her, and I still don't.

## Chapter Three

# Monday Monday

Mondays were good. They shouldn't have been really, not with the slog of the week ahead and Simon going back to work leaving Cassie and Will in their flat in the sky. But no, Mondays were good.

Cassie had Simon's packed lunch ready for him.

"There's no need you know. I could go to the canteen." Simon protested as Cassie pushed the plastic box and thermos flask towards him.

"I want you eating properly," Cassie insisted. "I don't want my hunk of a man, eating greasy canteen chips."

"They don't do greasy canteen chips; they do spicy chilli and feta salads."

"Well, you've got some cheddar and pickle in wholemeal bread. Eat it all up and grow into a big strong boy."

Simon laughed and took the packed lunch. "Honestly, Cass, what would I do without you?"

"Without me? You'd have half the lasses in Yorkshire running after you."

"Only half? More than that, surely."

"Oi! Big head! Get yourself to work and stop flattering yourself."

"Okay, work it is. Kiss?"

"Kiss."

He put his lunch back down on the worktop, wrapped his arms around Cassie, kissed her then squeezed her buttocks. "I could ring in to work. Tell them I've come down with something."

Cassie laughed now as well. "Come *up* with something more like. Say goodbye to your big son and then get yourself off to work. Earn some money to keep me in the style to which I've become accustomed."

"You're a hard woman. I'm on my way. Love you."

"Love you too."

Yes, Mondays were good. They were a time to restore order: get Simon off to work, see to Will and then set off together for St John's Mums and Toddlers. They went every week to the brightly painted annexe of St John's Church where Mums and babies converged. It was a precious hour or two where mums could get a cup of tea and a chat. Occasionally, there would be talks and demonstrations; a speaker from the National Childbirth Trust had recently visited, as had a Health Visitor, both of them offering sound, practical advice in a no-nonsense style, winning over the mums with empathy and a fund of good-natured stories. Cassie enjoyed these visits; she enjoyed the opportunity to sit Will on her knee and smile at him while she listened to the informal address. Most of all though she enjoyed the cup of tea and the nattering, she enjoyed the shared pride of the mums in their offspring and their achievements. She looked out particularly for Stacey, mother of Bethany, whom she'd first met and clicked with immediately at Mums and Toddlers. Stacey, she knew, sometimes found things difficult; didn't they all? But she lacked the art of assuming a placid exterior and what you saw with Stacey was what you got: no artifice, no pretence.

Whereas some mums arrived in style, smoothly pushing in the buggies and lifting out immaculate babies or toddlers dressed in family magazine fashion chic, Stacey, when she arrived that morning, looked as though the last forty-eight hours had been rough. Cassie's smile soon dropped when she met her.

"Stace! How's things?" It was a redundant question as Stacey's face, blotched and drawn, told the whole story.

"Don't ask, Cassie, don't ask. I'm blocked up with cold and so is she." She nodded at Bethany who, sure enough, needed a face wipe. Cassie plucked out a tissue and did the necessary.

"You shouldn't really have come today if you've both got colds."

It was an easy-going arrangement at Mums and Toddlers, no obligation, no requirement to be punctual, just the occasional gentle suggestion that the mums might like to come to a Sunday family service. They also asked the mums to be considerate over bugs and illnesses. Don't bring in germs to share with everyone else.

"I know," admitted Stacey, "but I've been up all night again seeing to her. I knew the best chance of settling her was to get out and walk her. And I needed to get out as well."

Cassie had never asked too much about Stacey's background. She knew she was bringing up Bethany by herself, living in her mum's house where there was a host of siblings, lots of noise and very little peace.

"Well, you're here now and you were right about Bethany." Cassie indicated the sleeping baby lying back open-mouthed. Each deep, breath was accompanied by a tiny rattle, like the snore of a sleeping lion cub. "You maybe ought to get her to a doctor, Stace; that might be more than a cold; she may have a chest infection."

No answer from Stacey and when Cassie turned to her, she realised she was close to breaking point, barely suppressing her sobbing.

"Come on." Cassie said, taking her hand. "Let's sort this."

Bethany and Will were content. It was acceptable to ask the other mothers to keep an eye on each other's children for a few minutes as odds and ends were attended to. Some mums took the opportunity to slip out for a fag.

"Can you keep an eye on these two?" Cassie called. "We'll do kettle duty this morning. Tea in five minutes."

"Good idea," someone replied and Cassie led Stacey in to the quiet kitchen area.

"Now let's get that kettle on." It was an idle remark, a way of overcoming awkwardness and silence, and it was also an unnecessary remark. Stacey wasn't interested in niceties; she threw her arms around Cassie and wept, pouring out a torrent of barely intelligible woes and Cassie stood bearing the physical load of the distraught girl draped over her and the weight of emotion.

"There, there." Cassie stroked and gently patted Stacey's back. "It can't be that bad, surely?"

However bad it was, it was the moment that Stacey needed. All the pressure was unloaded and the dark tunnel into which she had involuntarily strayed now had a chink of light.

"What is it, Stacey? What is it?"

It seemed like an age until Stacey regained any kind of coherence. Having loosened the straps of the weight around her shoulders she bundled it aside and began to breathe more freely.

"I'm sorry, Cassie. I don't know what came over me. Everything just suddenly became too much; coping with Bethany I mean, we're all on top of each other at home, I never seem to get any sleep, I never seem to get anything done, my life just seems to be spinning out of control and I lurch from one crisis to the next. Thank God for this place. Thank God for you."

Cassie led Stacey over to a row of orange plastic seats and they both sat down beneath a picture of Jesus, meek and mild, framed by a halo with his arms open in welcome. The title read: *Suffer the children.* Around the picture, Sunday School kids had pinned up their own work: huge sheets of sugar paper with painted imprints of hands, and there was a gloriously poster-painted rainbow with its own awkward lettering underneath: *A rainbow is God's smile.*

"Everybody feels that way, Stace. From time to time at least, it's not like the tv ads, is it? It's not all smiling mums and gurgling babies. Look at some of that lot out there. They might turn up with their turbo-charged four by four buggies with their kids in fashionably distressed denim, but they all face the terror of organising daily life."

Finally, Stacey broke into the beginnings of a smile. "Honestly, Cass. What are you like? *Fashionably distressed denim!* I've got some distressed denim, but it's not fashionable."

"That's better." They were both smiling now. "It's tough, Stace, but it's not impossible. I'll tell you what though, if your Bethany likes being pushed in the buggy, we should meet up and walk together. Will loves a long walk. Simon and I take him round the park at weekends. We'll do the same."

Stacey liked the idea. It was simple but it was exactly what she wanted but maybe it was too good an idea ever to happen.

"Cassie, it's okay for you, isn't it?" She didn't mean this bitterly. "You've got your own place. You've got your fella coming home every night. I bet you can put Will to bed at night and the pair of you can sit back and watch whatever you want on tv. I don't mean this nastily or anything, but I bet things have always fallen easily for you. I bet you were good at school; brainy, a big success and everything."

For the first time during this exchange, Cassie wobbled, caught unprepared and unable to mask the fright which passed across her face.

"Oh, Stacey, no! If you only knew the half of it..."

Now Stacey was perturbed by the unwitting damage she'd caused, exposing such a raw nerve. She wanted to make amends.

"I'm sorry. What have I said?" She repeated her apology. "I went too far, didn't I?"

"No, you're fine." Cassie had recovered. "Someday I'll tell you everything, but not yet, not yet."

Stacey, still anxious reached for Cassie's hand. "Cassie, we can be friends, can't we?"

Cassie squeezed her hand in return. "We *are* friends, Stace, we are friends."

"Now then, you two." Marion Bickerstaffe walked briskly into the kitchen oblivious to the emotional exchange which had recently taken place. She had an organiser role at Mums and Toddlers and she liked to be jolly; she liked to be in charge and she liked these mums; little more than young girls most of them. "Any sign of this tea?"

Cassie started guiltily. "Oh gosh! No, sorry. We haven't even started; we got caught up in a natter."

Brisk or not, Marion was not insensitive and she now gauged a little of what might have taken place; a look at Stacey's sunshine-after-the-rain smile gave a clue. "Well, not to worry. I'll pop back in and sort it. What I'd like you two to do is to come and meet our new volunteer. She's taking a year out before university and she'll be helping us on Mondays. Come on."

Cassie and Stacey swapped a furtive smile at each other as they trooped out behind Marion to meet the new helper who stood at the ready to take on any task that might come her way; the new helper who was enthusiastic and willing.

"Here they are." Marion was in full jolly mode as she marched up to the newcomer. "They were hiding in the kitchen. This is Cassie and Stacey; let me introduce you to…"

Cassie interrupted before the introductions were complete. "Hello, Alison."

"You two know each other?"

"Yes, we know each other."

## Chapter Four

# Don't Make a Fuss

Of course, they knew each other. Cassie Jackson and Alison Jones, hadn't it always been that way? Their friendship had been tighter than a knot in a wet rope, tight enough for each of them to know what the other was thinking and about to say; tight enough for them to produce punchlines simultaneously. Cassie couldn't think about Alison without smiling, or shuddering, come to that, often issuing an audible groan when she recalled the terrible split and the final family forum in Alison's house where her mother, Mrs Jones, eyes blazing, had uttered clenched-jaw pronouncements on Cassie's disgrace. And Cassie had borne it all, determined not to cry, determined to see it all through now she had got that far.

Yes, she often thought of Alison and she often felt the sharp shaft of pain. She thought of Alison when she was walking around the flat talking to herself, admiring her handiwork and saying, "Now what will Alison think of that?" When she was dealing with Will in one-sided conversations, she would make comparisons, "Of course, you'll be as big and strong as your Daddy, and as clever as Aunty Alison." But these were the only conversations she could have as talks with Simon about his family soon foundered and her own mum wouldn't dwell on the subject preferring to hide behind a façade of busyness: "Look, I'll just give this carpet a quick once-over." Cassie's solitary outlet had been an unexpected meeting with old Mrs Neal.

Had it been the blue sky or the invigorating wind which had compelled Cassie to wheel Will the long way home from Babies and Toddlers? Was it just an impulse for a little more exercise or was there some compulsion to face up to her demons? Either way, Cassie had pushed the buggy around once familiar streets right up to the perimeter fencing of Manor Hall School where nothing appeared to have changed. Judging by the number of cars in the car park, the school was in session. Some lights were lit but there was no visible activity and no noise. A banner had been strung across a section of fencing, "Manor Hall School: a good and improving school." It was more than Cassie was ready for. She pushed the buggy beyond the school grounds and sat on the nearest garden wall to take some deep breaths and ease the tightness in her chest, oblivious of the face that watched her from beyond the net curtains in the terraced house. For once she didn't carry out her monologue for Will as almost doubled up, she could only concentrate on taking in those deep breaths and exhaling slowly. What had she been thinking about?

"Are you all right, love?" The old lady's sudden appearance startled Cassie.

"Yes, thank you. I just needed a sit down, that's all. Is this your wall? I'm sorry."

The woman looked at her closely. "It's Cassandra Jackson, isn't it? You might not remember me…Annie Neal…I used to work with your mum a long time ago."

Cassie gave a thin smile. She didn't think she did remember but Annie Neal peered into the buggy and continued, "And this is who all the fuss was about."

"What fuss?" Cassie regained some of her fight and made to stand up. Her testy response was over-emphatic.

"Well, it was always a fuss in my day, I don't suppose it has changed all that much."

Cassie found herself apologising again but there was no harm done.

"I was going to offer you a glass of water but I think a cup of tea would be a better idea. You've got ten minutes and the kettle is already on."

Cassie had wanted to refuse politely but she found herself guiding the buggy up a stone step and into the house straight into the front room which told of a life lived. The furniture was dated and comfortable, a big clock on the fireplace issued sonorous ticks and every spare place was utilised for showing framed photographs.

"That's my Gordon, God bless him."

"And that's you, you look lovely!" Cassie's admiration of the faded wedding photograph was unaffected.

"Thank-you, dear. There was a time, there was a time." Annie smiled wistfully as Cassie picked up a number of other photographs, standard issue school photographs of succeeding generations. Annie did her best to identify to name each of the smiling faces and provide some autobiographical detail but sometimes this eluded her.

"Do you see a lot of them?" Cassie asked.

"Families grow up and move away, but they should stay in touch."

Cassie looked again at the array of grinning kids, uniforms and school photograph poses. Grandkids and great-grandkids who had long since flown this particular nest, who now roosted in different trees and flew freely over distant landscapes. She shuddered, and for no particular reason, checked that the sleeping Will was well wrapped up.

She looked again at Annie Neal, her kindly stoic face and the tidy room in which she had been invited to sit. She thought about the house in a terraced row built over a hundred years ago easily, the street outside ill-equipped to deal with modern traffic and the twice daily routine of jams and obstructions as the school run was underway. She thought of her own flat, six floors up into the sky in a monstrous block and the realisation dawned on her that both the house and the flat were stalked by the ghost of loneliness.

It was there where Cassie realised that there was little point in trying to drink her tea and eat her biscuit quickly and get off as Annie

Neal's invitation for a five- minute sit down could be extended indefinitely and it was there, cornered by the old lady's kindness and loneliness, where Cassie sat back and for the first time told her whole story.

A cup of tea and a digestive biscuit helps of course, but Cassie had found an old friend of her mother who listened, who did not judge and didn't issue pronouncements. With the telling, Cassie was able to unload the weight she had carried for so long. She had been wronged, she had done some bad things herself, but in her tale, she sought neither approval nor sympathy, she simply let it flow, letting in some light on her dark secret and Annie Neal listened until Cassie finally reached the end and, apart from the ticking of the clock and the muffled roar of the traffic outside, the room fell to silence.

It was some time until the silence was broken. "I'm an old woman Cassandra, I'm in my seventies. I was born during the war. I always felt that I lived through some hard times. We didn't have much, Gordon and I, only the hope that things would get better, for our kids, if not for us. But I don't know that they ever have. Hitler's bombs? I don't remember Hitler's bombs. You've told me about things which must be worse than Hitler's bombs."

Cassie made a point of adjusting Will's blankets again. He'd slept through Cassie's long tale but now he was becoming restless. Cassie too was uncomfortable, why had she opened up to this old woman? She had said too much.

"There's nothing I can do," Annie continued, "No magic wand I can wave. You young people hug now, don't you? I can't even do that. We just had to carry on and not make a fuss."

Cassie smiled. "You've listened to me and that's been important. Thank-you."

"Well, I'm always happy to listen. Don't be so hard on yourself, Cassie. There's no reason why you should take the blame." Cassie looked doubtfully at her. "I mean it. You've got a whole life in front of you to live *and* someone else who will be learning from you."

Cassie looked down at Will who looked to be on the verge of waking fully and beginning to shout for a feed. She was well aware of her responsibilities to him but Annie had reminded her that she had her own life to live as well. How often had her own future disappeared from view submerged beneath a prospect of washing, feeding and caring?

"And come round again. It's been a long time since there has been a baby in this house." There was both invitation and pleading in her voice.

Cassie thought about the journey she had taken to reach the house, the walk past the school which had left her physically sick, the narrow pavements with the heavy traffic rushing past and then the great well of loneliness which existed inside the front door.

"Yes, I'd like that." Cassie stood up. "And there's something I'd like to do for you."

"What's that love?"

"A hug, a young person's hug."

## Chapter Five

# Dreamworld

"And the winner is...Cassie Jackson!"

Wave after wave of applause rolled forward from the excited audience. Several times she tried to speak but she was engulfed by further rapturous applause. She smiled and waved and beckoned for silence but still they clapped and roared and called out her name.

"Cass-ie, Cass-ie..."

Embarrassed now she shuffled inside her sparkling evening dress and then leaned forward to speak directly into the microphone.

"Thank-you, thank-you."

Gradually order was resumed. Those who had stood to applaud, hands above their heads, sat down again and all the stars from the world of pop music, television and film sitting around the candle-lit tables were poised to hear what she had to say. Illuminated in the spotlight, smiling and clutching a statuette she cleared her throat and began again.

"To stand here and look around and see all the people who I have admired for years, people who are featured in my own music collection at home...I have to tell you that you people owe me a lot of pocket money."

Another interruption with warm laughter this time.

"To see you people sitting there and to know that you've voted my album as album of the year," she held the statuette aloft, "is a choking experience."

Her voice faltered with emotion, "I can only say that you have made me a very proud fourteen-year-old. Thank you all so much."

* * * * *

Cassie Jackson was a dreamer. Just ask anyone who knew her: teachers, friends, mum and dad. Cassie? Yeah, a bit of a dreamer. Lives in a land of dreams.

It was Alison who nudged her back to life. "Cassie! Stop daydreaming. Come on, let's get this finished."

Around them the classroom hummed with chatter, gossip and a little work activity. Given the chance, Cassie and Alison always worked together. Their desks were pushed alongside each other in the corner where the History display on the Victorian age was slowly taking shape on the notice board. From a poster Queen Victoria stared down at the various efforts of the class.

"If we don't get this finished, you know what she'll say." Alison indicated to the sombre looking monarch.

"No, what will she say?"

Alison adopted a deep tone for greater effect, "We are not amused."

"She never really said that, you know." Cassie had read as much.

"She didn't?"

"No," said Cassie. "All a myth apparently. You can tell by looking at her, can't you? That trendy black outfit. It's obvious that she was a laugh a minute."

They enjoyed the joke and settled down to some work but Cassie soon broke the silence.

"Ali? What do you think of my award winning, multi-million selling debut C.D.?"

"You what?"

"You know, my triple platinum C.D. Dreamworld."

"Oh that! The one where you wrote all of the songs yourself. The one that has catapulted you to world fame – the most famous teenager on the planet."

"That's the one."

Alison smiled. "It's okay I suppose."

"Just okay? Are you sure you're not a little bit jealous?"

"No, I'm not jealous. Just give me a lift home in your chauffeur driven Roller and I'll be okay."

Cassie smiled too. "Imagine that, Alison Jones, school netball captain, dance champion and coolest girl in Manor Hall School, jealous of Little Old Cassie Jackson."

"Little Old Cassie Jackson will soon be getting us both a detention," Alison said, "if she doesn't stop daydreaming about mega stardom."

There were times when Cassie took the daydreaming thing too far. Why was she always doing that?

## Chapter Six

# 1854: Manor Hall Farm

Will sat in the old barn as the daylight faded. The last rays of the sun slanted across the floor catching particles of dust, illuminating them like moths around a lamp. Summer was coming to an end and Will knew it would be his last on Manor Hall Farm, his place of employment and that of his father and his grandfather before that. At sixteen years of age, he was answering the call of his Queen and country.

Without him life would continue on the farm, the harvest would be brought in, the winter feed would be stored and, in due time, the spring lambing would take place. Manor Hall Farm would live on much as it had ever done. Will knew he was needed in the Crimea to fight the Russian Bear.

A wide wooden door at the far end of the barn creaked slowly open and dazzling light flooded in. A black silhouette stood framed in the doorway.

"Will?"

"I'm in here, Joe."

"I thought I might find you here."

Still struggling to adjust his eyes to the darkness in the barn, Joseph Graham hesitantly made his way towards the voice. He took his friend's hand and shook it. Words were difficult between them.

"Still going then?"

"No choice now, Joe lad. Tomorrow, I become one of Her Majesty's finest."

Joe shook his head doubtfully. "It may not be too late. My father knows people. He has influence."

But Will was determined. "I don't need your father's influence, Joe. Our country is at war. Don't you think this is a fine thing that I'm doing?"

Joe made no reply. Somewhere in the far distance a bird sang.

"Well Joe," Will persisted, "don't you think this is a fine thing I'm doing?"

Joe, standing less than a yard from his friend, faced him squarely. "No Will, no I don't. Let other people go and fight. You should stay right here." Will made to interrupt him but Joe silenced him with a gesture. "Someday all of this farm will be mine. I'll extend the estate. Anything is possible. It'll be the best-run farm in the whole of the county, the best-run farm because I'll have the best manager. You, Will. You can be my manager and together we will be the envy of every farmer and landowner who hears about Manor Hall Farm. We will live in a land of dreams.

Will shook his head slowly. "I've spent all of my life on this farm. I know every inch of it and I've worked through all of the seasons here. I know the animals and I know the jobs. But I also know you're already in a land of dreams. They don't make managers out of the likes of me. Me and my type were born to labour Joe. And when you are the owner, I'll know my place, don't worry."

Once again Joe struggled for words. Will had touched upon the very subject about which they never spoke. Throughout all of their friendship; sixteen years of running in the fields, swimming in the river and wrestling in the barn, they had never acknowledged the great gulf that lay between them until now and Will's words.

"And besides," Will broke the silence, "Everything tells me that this is the right thing to do. It will make a man of me, Joe. Our Lucy says I should go. She says she sees me in a smart uniform with a pretty girl close by my side."

Joe shook his head ruefully thinking of Lucy with her jet-black hair and piercing blue eyes. "Your Lucy! Her and her visions. Tell her we don't believe in mumbo jumbo. We don't believe in witch-hunts anymore either. Tell her she's lucky not to be on a ducking stool."

But Joe's light-hearted banter lacked conviction. He couldn't articulate the real words he wanted to say to his friend. "I've brought you something Will. A present." Awkwardly he thrust a small object towards his friend. "I've had it inscribed Will. Let it speak for me while we're apart."

There was nothing else to say and to stay any longer, Joe knew, would be unmanly. As suddenly as he had arrived, he left again, through the creaking door into the sunlit golden field, back towards the big house of Manor Hall Farm. Will remained in the barn fingering a small silver snuff box and tracing the inscription engraved upon it. Too dark in the barn of course but he could make out seven words. And the second word began with W. Will. Yes, Will, his own name.

## Chapter Seven

# Manor Hall School

Cassie and Alison were best friends and had been for years. They sat together in school, they spent hours at each other's houses and they unwrapped and shared the deepest of secrets. But sometimes, Cassie would fix her piercing blue eyes on Alison and shoot a look of helpless hatred. It wasn't Cassie's fault that Alison was perfect. Everyone knew that Alison was perfect except Alison herself of course who would never admit to such a thing. But Cassie knew it and other people measured themselves by standards set by Alison.

Teachers enjoyed searching for superlatives to place upon Alison's report and "excellent", "first-class" and "a pleasure to teach" was often written. The choir leader thrilled to hear her pure notes. Even the boys paid respect; for Cassie they would shout and ask her to join in their games of football, but for Alison they would stop the game as she passed by. Not for her the world of being teased or suffering embarrassment. Alison wasn't clumsy, nor did she make daft remarks.

What's more, Alison was clever; very clever. She always got good marks and she received excellent grades as a matter of habit. Jokingly Cassie had once suggested some sabotage.

"One of these times you ought to write some nonsense."

"What do you mean?"

"Well for a Geography project you could write about sheep farming in central London."

Alison laughed. "Or the Yorkshire pineapple growing industry."

Cassie was delighted. "Oh yes do! Miss Jenkins will still give you an A grade." She began to mimic their class teacher, "A remarkable response children."

And Alison joined in, "Delightful sensitivity." Then they both nodded their heads to shake imaginary hair out of their eyes before falling together in laughter.

Alison continued to smile for some time afterwards knowing that such sabotage would never happen. Yes, Alison was perfect; Miss Goody Two Shoes, but one day, Cassie would be best in the class, she would glow in warm praise from teachers, and she would be the centre of attention in the school yard. Yes, one day, but until then Cassie had to live in the long shadow cast by Alison and the other dread about which she found it impossible to speak to anyone.

But Cassie too had a special gift; a gift so special and so disturbing that she was definitely keeping it to herself. How could she tell anyone that from time to time without warning an unusual feeling would come over her? That she would get a tingling inside, a little dizziness, a feeling that she was beginning to float in the air and then the visions would appear? Slowly at first, like a foggy day clearing, the images would gradually form and people, often people that she knew or sometimes complete strangers, would be going about their daily business and Cassie would get a glimpse into their lives. They were fantasies, dreams and slices of life that were all too real.

"There's Cassie daydreaming again," people would say but these were frightening times. Dreaming about winning pop music awards was one thing but what could these other visions possibly mean? And why was Cassie singled out to receive them? Were they trying to tell her something? Whatever the reason, it was something Cassie was determined to keep to herself. Would anyone believe her? The opportunity to start a teasing campaign would be far too great.

"Cassie Jackson has voices speaking in her head."

"She lives in a dream world."

She wouldn't breathe a word of this to anyone, not even Alison, her best friend and sharer of secrets. Not all secrets can be shared.

The school hall was packed for assembly. Class by class, followed by their stern looking teachers, had marched in dutifully, mindful of the No Talking Rule. As everyone settled, Mr Brown, the Headteacher switched off the music and made his way to a central point where everyone could see and hear him.

"Thank-you everyone. This morning's piece of music. Does anyone know what it is?"

No-one did. Mr Brown's gaze swept expectantly around the assembly hall. The younger children, sitting at the front did not know. Mr Brown looked towards the older children at the back.

"Well? Any suggestions?"

Still no-one spoke although the teachers looked intently, hoping that someone from their class would get the answer right. No-one did so Mr Brown continued.

"That was the final movement from Beethoven's Sixth Symphony, his Pastoral. It is the point at which the shepherds celebrate after the storm."

Mr Brown beamed. There was no doubt about it: he liked his job and he liked assemblies. He liked to have the children listening to the music and to what he had to say. "Today's music is very appropriate because today we are involved in a celebration of our own. Today we celebrate the hard work done by Miss Jenkins' class in their History project. Miss Jenkins…?"

Cassie sat surrounded by her classmates. Any minute now the presentation would take place and all of the children would applaud. Cassie allowed herself a small smile of satisfaction. It spread a warm glow of happiness inside her.

"Cassie! Cassie Jackson!"

"Yes, Miss Jenkins?"

"Have I got your full and undivided attention?"

Startled, Cassie looked around at the familiar walls of the classroom and her classmates staring at her hoping for a minor diversion to the day's events.

"Yes Miss."

"Well thank you for that. Anyone could be forgiven for thinking that you were daydreaming."

Several smirks were exchanged amongst the class at the thought of Cassie Jackson daydreaming. This was one of Miss Jenkins' familiar jibes. But the teacher turned away and resumed her lesson.

Alison turned to Cassie and risked a whisper. "You were miles away."

"Yeah, sort of. Listen Ali, did we have assembly today?"

"No, not on Thursdays, why?"

"Oh nothing. Just something I was thinking about that's all."

Alison smiled. If her friend was spending time thinking about assemblies there was something seriously wrong.

## Chapter Eight

# The Competition

Miss Jenkins needed the full attention of the class because she had something important to announce. She chose to reveal details about the History project competition during a lesson where the clocks appeared to have stopped. The sun shone and the classroom was bathed in a drowsiness that lulled minds and bodies. Miss Jenkins knew what she was doing. The summer term stretched ahead long and languid and the class needed pepping up before a sleepiness curled up and settled down on all of the pupils.

She gave a shake of her head to move her hair out of her eyes. "There will be a small prize awarded to the project that I consider to be the best." She dangled the carrot tantalisingly and once again Cassie caught a brief picture of the packed assembly hall and Mr Brown, smiling and presenting a prize.

No amount of begging or pleading would persuade Miss Jenkins to reveal further details. No, the prize would not be the usual Mars Bar. No, she would not tell the class exactly what the prize would be.

"This project is important in its own right." Miss Jenkins had a weakness for the portentous statement, "It has intrinsic value."

It was true. Prize winning for Cassie would only be the icing on the cake. She set to work on her project on Florence Nightingale with so much hard work and care she could have been the nurse herself. She spent hours on internet sites, she gathered information from weighty encyclopaedias, maps were carefully copied and illustrations were lovingly drawn. After school she made several visits to the town library, consulted CD Roms and paid to make printouts of biographical details of the famous nurse and her work during the Crimean War.

Cassie was going to win the competition. She wanted her project to be the best and she wouldn't be denied for lack of effort or devotion. Even Alison was surprised.

The big advantage of living in the same avenue is that you can pop in and out of your friend's house. Alison called at Cassie's to invite her to tea. They could also mess around for a while until it was ready, perhaps watch some t.v. But Cassie said no. Quite rudely Alison thought although she didn't say anything. Cassie wanted to work on her History project and didn't want to be disturbed.

"It's not due in for another week." protested Alison. But Cassie was adamant. She had seen a vision of the future; she had seen Mr Brown beaming and heard all of the children clapping. She had to continue on the project. To Alison she merely said, "You can stay around if you want."

Work in progress impressed Alison. She flicked through the folder of immaculate handwriting and fingered gently the protective tracing paper over neat maps and diagrams. The loving detail was impossible to ignore, every page was a picture of care and attention.

Gently placing the project back on the desk, Alison began to shift around the bedroom picking up odds and ends. Her plan of giggling together over her mum's monster burgers and chips had been ruined and now she was at a loose end. She leafed through a sketch book.

"Are these your drawings?" she asked admiringly.

"Yes, but they're not very good." said Cassie glowing.

"Yes, they are. Look at this cat curled up by the fire. He looks ever so snug and warm."

But Cassie wanted to change the subject. "What are you doing for the project?"

"Oh something on Victorian writers," Alison replied casually. "You know, some of the poets, Tennyson and Arnold, "Morte D'Arthur", "Dover Beach" and all that stuff. Pretty boring really."

Cassie said nothing, but she thought of her Florence Nightingale walking up and down the darkened hospital wards bathed in the soft light from her lamp, gently comforting the wounded soldiers. She could hear her whispered words and feel the sense of relief felt by the men. She was a national heroine and an inspiration to thousands of girls. As for Alison's poets, Cassie had never even heard of them.

## Chapter Nine

# A Land of Dreams

Alison continued to root around the bedroom, flicking through some magazines and then checking out a rack of CDs. Cassie was not to be distracted. Alison sighed and she was about to make her excuses for leaving when the object on the bedside table caught her eye.

"What's this?" she said picking it up and holding it to the light. Cassie looked up from her desk.

"It's a snuff box."

"A what? A snuff box? What's one of them?"

Cassie smiled and affected a posh accent. "A snuff box is a box for holding one's snuff."

But Alison was not to be put off. "Great! Now I know. Is it gold? Is it valuable?"

It was no good. Cassie was not going to be allowed to continue with her project. She put down her pen, rose from her desk and walked across to take hold of the small box.

"No, it's not gold. It needs a good polish and it may be silver but I doubt if it valuable. It's been in our family for ages apparently. Look carefully underneath and you'll see the inscription. Look here."

Alison looked to where Cassie was pointing and there sure enough was an inscription in neat writing. She began to read. "To Will and the Land of Dreams." She looked at Cassie. "That's amazing. Who's Will? And where is the Land of Dreams?"

"Search me," said Cassie. "That thing's been in our family for ages and no one's ever heard of a Will."

Alison was very taken by the find. It was a mystery that needed solving. "You ought to do some research and find out the full story," she told her friend. "After all, where there's a Will, there's a way."

## Chapter Ten

# For Queen and Country

All History projects to be handed in the following day with no excuses accepted for lateness. No problem for Cassie. She sat alone in her bedroom reading through her finished project for a final time. The hours she'd spent, the care and attention she'd lavished upon her work. She turned over the final page and weighed the satisfying bulk of material in her hands before she hugged the whole project close to her chest.

And then in the darkness that suddenly closed in around her she felt a tingling feeling and a dizziness before a hazy fog began to clear...

* * * * *

"Nurse! Nurse!" The call came from in amongst the moans and grumblings of the darkened ward. The nurse held her lamp and picked her way through the smells and groans, the beds and bodies that lay on every available space on the floor.

"What is it, Soldier?"

Her lamp shone on the pale face of a young boy. Seventeen? Sixteen?

"Could we...do you think you could talk to me for a few minutes? He lay uncomfortably on the bed and struggled with his words.

"Talk? There are hundreds of wounded soldiers here. I haven't got time for talking." But she saw his painful grimace and checked her impatience. "We're doing what we can for you. There may be a doctor coming round tomorrow and we are also hoping for some stew. That will soon have you on your feet again, Soldier."

He twisted his body painfully in order to face her more directly. "Please, call me Will. What's your name?"

She lowered her voice even further. "We are not allowed to give out our names. We're here to nurse."

He looked at her again and smiled weakly. "This is no place for a young girl."

And she smiled, thinking much the same thing about him and the hundreds, no thousands, like him. The countless young boys, who had been killed, maimed and wounded.

"You need some sleep. Get your strength back." She made to move away.

"No, Nurse. Wait please." There was desperation in his failing voice. "There's something in my tunic pocket that I need."

Around her the moans continued. Some of the wounded cried out in agony, not knowing what it was they said, not knowing when their pain would end. Others relived the horrors of the battlefield, opening up wounds that they would carry long after physical scars had healed.

"I shouldn't stay here." She told him. "I might get into trouble." But something about the pleading look in his eyes sent her searching through the pockets of the mud-spattered soldier's tunic that hung by the bed. At first, she thought the pockets were empty but then her fingers came upon a small box.

"Is this it? A snuff box?"

He was trying to lean forward to see then he relaxed his efforts.

"That's the one. Given to me by my friend Joe." Slowly the anxiety seemed to be leaving his tensed body. "We've been friends all of our lives and spent all that time on the same farm. Joe was the best at everything, running, swimming, wrestling. I could never beat him at anything. That's why I joined up. I wanted to do something that Joe hadn't done. So, I did it. I joined the army."

He paused as if gathering strength for further details. "I can tell him now, can't I? I can tell him that I fought for Queen and Country at the Battle of Balaklava."

She laid a soothing hand on his brow. "Yes, you can tell him. But you really must get some rest now."

But weak as his voice was, he continued. "There's some writing on the box, underneath, there's some writing."

She held the box close to the light of her lamp and peered at it. Sure enough, there was a delicate inscription.

"Read it to me please." Again, the anxiety and the pleading note had returned to his voice and it dawned on her suddenly that this young boy who had spent all of his life on an English farm, who was constantly losing out to his best friend at running, swimming and wrestling, and who now lay badly wounded in a military hospital thousands of miles from home, could not read. He could not read the inscription that his friend had had written on his present. She peered closely at the underside of the box and then told him, "It says, "To Will and the Land of Dreams."

He lay back finally content, so much so that she thought the effort had taken him to sleep. She leaned over him to check and she heard him whisper, "He always said that one day we'd run the whole farm, we'd live in a land of dreams." He gave a wan smile. "It's yours."

She could barely hear what he was saying. "What did you say?"

There was no mistaking him the second time. "I said it's yours. The box. Keep it."

They weren't allowed to take anything from wounded soldiers. It was strictly against regulations but she didn't want to cause him any further distress. She waited until his eyes were definitely closed and then slipped the box back into his tunic pocket.

"Good night, Will," she whispered to the sleeping boy. She would come and speak to him again in the morning.

She didn't speak to him in the morning. She couldn't. Will had died and another young boy whose leg had been shattered just below the thigh by a Russian cannonball had taken his bed.

## Chapter Eleven

# The Presentation

It was the big day; the one Cassie had worked towards for so long, the day that History projects had to be handed in. On time spent and application alone she deserved to win the prize. But doubt now crowded her certainty. Her latest vision had left her anxious. It had been so vivid, so clear and so disturbing.

"Cassie love, are you alright?" Cassie's mum leaned across the breakfast table.

"Yeah, sure." Cassie roused herself from her preoccupations.

"Well, have a piece of toast then." Nothing could be wrong with the world if people had a healthy appetite.

"No thanks, Mum. I've had sufficient."

Turning down breakfast raised suspicions in Cassie's mum.

"Cassandra, you are all right, aren't you?"

"Yes Mum. Please don't nag."

She looked searchingly at her daughter, at her shining black hair and piercing blue eyes.

"You're so lucky you know, to have your father's hair and eyes. There must be generations of the Jackson family with those looks. Jet black hair and blue eyes to die for."

Cassie squirmed in her seat, anxious to finish breakfast and be off to school.

"You are looking pale though love. Are you sickening for something?"

"Mum!" Cassie was close to losing her cool completely. "I've told you, I'm all right."

It was her standard response, "I'm all right," or "I'm okay," often followed with "Leave me alone." Mrs Jackson began to fret again about Cassie who used to be so lively and joyful; her bouncy daughter who used to take such pleasure in all manner of things. Now she was deadly intense and although she was so quick-witted and had her own sense of humour, she kept these qualities hidden preferring a scathing comment about anyone being flippant or casual. Yet she herself often seemed to be miles away, living some other kind of existence. Where was her beautiful daughter? Where was the girl of a few years ago who was such fun when her father was around? Guiltily, Mrs Jackson put the thought from her mind. It was too easy to blame her husband; when marriages founder, the children suffer and both parents should share the responsibility, and yes, the guilt. Mrs Jackson's guilt was evident in her need for constant assurance. It was far too close to nagging, she knew, but she couldn't rid herself of the solid conviction that her daughter needed help.

"I just need to know that you're all right."

"Mum!" Cassie's patience was being stretched to a dangerously thin point.

Cassie tried to calm herself. Was she alright? She felt fine, although she would feel a lot better if she didn't have a recurring image of Will, a sixteen-year-old Private in the Queen's army. Will who had signed up to defend the Empire and also to score a point against his best friend. Because the one thing that Will hadn't said but which had been as clear as daylight was that none of it had been worth it: the competition with his friend, the act of bravado in signing up to join the army and the fighting in a country, miles away from home, had all been worthless. Throughout the night Cassie had seen the candle-white face of Will and heard his insistent whisper, "I can tell him now, can't I? I can tell him that I fought for Queen and country at the battle of Balaklava."

"Because if you're not feeling well enough you shouldn't be going to school." Cassie's mum again, anxious and concerned.

"I'm okay Mum. And I'm going to school because I hand in my history project today."

Of course, the History project. Cassie's mum had been aware of the act of devotion that had resulted in the finished project. She had read every last word and studied the immaculate diagrams. She was very impressed and, although she was reluctant to admit it, she was also slightly alarmed at the intensity that her daughter had shown. She looked at her pale face and the signs of strain under her eyes.

"You haven't overdone it have you love? I mean you haven't tired yourself with all of this homework, have you?"

"Mum! Cassie tried to keep the note of exasperation out of her voice. "You always tell me to work hard at school."

"Yes dear, but do it for the right reasons won't you?"

Cassie stood up abruptly from the breakfast table. The right reasons indeed! She didn't know what her mum was talking about. She wouldn't be saying things like that when the History prize was given out.

Presentation Day. Miss Jenkins stood in the assembly hall with a broad smile on her face and why not? Her plan had worked. The class had shown a lot of energy and the pile of projects was the result of some very hard work. She meant what she said, "The standard has been high and choosing the winner has been most difficult."

All of the classes had filed in and sat down. From the front of the hall, music played and Mr Brown stood and beamed before indicating that the music should be turned off. Then he made his way to a central point where everyone could see and hear him. He looked around at everyone gathered together. Some referred to this audience as young people or adults in the making. Students was a popular term, but not for fourteen-year-olds surely? Others, and he shuddered as he thought this, used the word *kids*. No, they were children, and in some respects, they were his children because that was his job – to know the children. And he did, despite the huge numbers that passed through these doors. Form tutors would get to know the thirty children in their form, subject teachers would get to know a few more through their lessons, the asking of questions, the checking of work and the collection of homework, but Mr Brown got to know them all. He read all of their reports, he added his own comments and he learned names. He couldn't put a name to every face obviously but a lot of them he could. Some children found their way to him as a matter of course; it was as inevitable as the rivers running into the sea that he should encounter them and vice versa as their school careers lurched through a succession of offences and retribution. Others were high flyers who needed only a clear flight path to eventual success and Mr Brown learned the names of these children because their success was the school's success and he needed to bandy names and affection with beaming parents at Parents' Evenings and other important events. Those who were good at sport and music also fell into this category. With winning teams and highly-praised concerts the school would continue to go from strength to strength and Mr Brown, who was now teaching the children of the children he once taught, could only find his position to be impregnable, his reputation continuing to spread amongst these houses, streets and avenues, from family to family and generation to generation. Yet there was another group of children he sought out, a group to which Mr Brown attached a great deal of importance. There were some children who didn't fit neatly into the earlier categories, some children who could drift through the net unless steps were taken and they were made to feel special. This was Mr Brown's particular gift; with his finely tuned antennae he could pick out the children who otherwise would become lost souls. Doubtless they had some talent or skill but they lacked something, something in their background, parents who didn't make a noise and demand the best for their delightful offspring perhaps. Take the Jackson girl for instance, the dark-haired girl in Year Nine with soulful blue eyes. She was reasonably bright and certainly not a trouble maker, but she wasn't operating in top gear and she wasn't producing of her best. She was given a lot to daydreaming. Family background? No brothers or sisters and her parents were separated. Now she had been a prime candidate to become one of Mr Brown's girls; another little task for Mr Brown. He beamed again, his well-practised beam. There was no doubt about it, he liked his job and he liked assemblies.

"Thank you everyone. Now then, this morning's piece of music, does anyone know what it is?"

There was silence now as Mr Brown looked enquiringly around the hall. No-one offered an answer. Cassie sat in amongst her classmates knowing for certain that they had all been listening to Beethoven – his sixth symphony. She knew this for a fact but said nothing. She could have gathered some cheap praise for knowing the answer to Mr Brown's question but she was there for a greater purpose, certain that she too would soon be standing at the front of the hall listening to the applause of all the pupils.

Mr Brown continued, "Today we are involved in a celebration of our own. Today we celebrate the hard work done by Miss Jenkins' class in their history project. Miss Jenkins...?

The assembled pupils were a mixture of impatience and expectation. Cassie especially fixed onto Miss Jenkins' every move unable to take her eyes away from her for even a second.

"I was so impressed," Miss Jenkins smiled and tossed her hair out of her face, "and I'm so pleased that Mr Brown has allowed us to make the presentation in assembly."

It was just as Cassie had seen it. Mr Brown stood at the front smiling broadly. The applause of the class would be next.

"So, without any more ado – the winner!" Miss Jenkins had wrung every last drop of tension out of the situation. "I'm going to award the prize to a project of delightful sensitivity. I doubt if I've ever read work of such of such a high standard on the Victorian period from pupils of your age. And if I may, I'd like to read a verse from the poet on whom the winning project is based."

And so, summoning up her feelings for language, Miss Jenkins began to read from "Dover Beach."

"Ah love let us be true

To one another! For the world, which seems

To lie before us like a land of dreams,

So various, so beautiful, so new,

Hath really neither joy, nor love, nor light,

Nor certitude, nor peace, nor help from pain."

She paused briefly to ensure that her dramatic reading was being appreciated. Years ago, in her college days, Miss Jenkins had been an actress. She remembered being a very tragic Ophelia. Now she was treating the assembly to a sample of her emotional range. She continued,

"And we are here as in a darkling plain

Swept with confused alarms of struggle and flight.

Where ignorant armies clash by night."

Sitting on the front row, her eyes filling, Cassie neither understood nor even heard a single word.

## Chapter Twelve

# Best Friends

They were walking home together from school largely in silence. Every attempt at conversation came to an abrupt halt. The summer holidays were approaching. Did Cassie have any plans? There was only a brief grunt by way of reply.

Alison held the gift token awarded for the best History project. She'd walked to the front of the assembly and smiled graciously as Mr Brown handed over the prize and the whole school had applauded.

"Stingy, eh?" She was trying to make a joke but she saw the pain and disappointment in Cassie's eyes. The glance told her that any words of consolation to her friend would sound hollow.

But Cassie's thoughts went deeper than Alison could ever imagine. She was thinking about friendship and competition. She was thinking about a young boy who had gone to fight and die in the Crimea to prove something to his best friend. She was thinking about a snuff box, a symbol of friendship that had been handed over for safe keeping and which now, almost a hundred and fifty years later, stood on her bedside table.

If the opportunity arose to compete with Alison again, she would resist. She would defer like a small boat giving way to an ocean liner and sail serenely in the wake, avoiding the buffets and swell. She would not expose herself and she would never ever again leave herself vulnerable because Cassie was uncomfortably aware that inside her something dark and malignant was growing. She has hoped it would go away, but no, there it was slowly enlarging: the thought that with all her success, all of her triumphs, Cassie's resentment of Alison was turning into a black knot of hate. How could you hate your best friend? What was happening to her when she knew in her heart, she had been a good girl once? It was like swimming in the sea and when you want to get out you want to go and sit on the golden sand, but there's a deep undercurrent dragging you back in, and as you get pulled deeper a vicious whirlpool waits to swallow you up for ever. Cassie had to draw on all of her strength to fight for the girl she had once been. It was the only piece of driftwood onto which she could cling.

Alison broke into Cassie's thoughts. "Look, when I go and choose a book, will you come and help me? Come on, please." Cassie looked towards her friend before she continued. "And will you do me another favour? Will you show me how to draw cats?"

She wanted to learn to draw cats? Cassie could certainly teach her. The trick was to get the eyes right. They would draw cats together; books full of cat pictures.

Cassie managed a fragile smile and nodded.

"Okay."

After all, they were best friends and had been for years.

## Chapter Thirteen

# The Whole World in her Hands

Chaos, absolute chaos in the corridor outside the changing rooms deep inside the Rose Bowl Stadium, Pasadena. Lights had been set up and in amongst the cheering and shouting a camera crew jostled to get the prized interview in the can. In the studio, the presenter made his smiling link,

"We can now go down to hear from Cassie Jackson, England's last-minute goal scoring hero."

Cassie, positioned in shot, quickly pushed the hair from her brow and wiped the sweat from her face with the palm of her hand in readiness.

"Cassie, the winning goal in the Women's World Cup Final. Has it sunk in yet?"

Cassie smiled. "Not really, no. All I know is that it wasn't just about me. The winners today are the group of mates who have worked very hard for just this moment, we've worked, we've trained and we've fought for what we wanted."

"Cassie!" A shower of champagne was sprayed in Cassie's direction and she took avoiding action before standing up again, smiling rueful apologies on behalf of her celebrating team mates, ready to take the next question.

"Cassie, if you look at this monitor, you could perhaps take us through the winning goal."

They were playing deep into time added on for stoppages, heading for extra time and, if no goals were scored, then a penalty shoot-out. There was no time left now for any drama before the shrill blast of the whistle would indicate the end of ninety minutes play in the Women's

World Cup Final. But Cassie appeared to have other ideas, there was time for one last dramatic twist and she set off on an energy-sapping run down the centre of the pitch. It all depended on Sammy on the left wing who had possession of the ball. If Sammy could work the ball on to her favoured left foot, if she could look up and see that Cassie had gained those vital metres of space, if she could deliver the inch-perfect ball? It was all "ifs", but Cassie responded to the slim chance, to the *what if* possibility. It was no time for gambling and Cassie was going to gamble.

Sammy made the connection; an innocuous looking cross-field pass with insufficient English support for it to pay dividends. But Cassie had made the lung-bursting run; if the move broke down, she'd be hopelessly out of position, but she wasn't thinking about that now. The tall, blonde American centre back was fractionally out of position, she couldn't attack the ball, she couldn't clear the danger with one hefty hoof down the field because Cassie was going to reach the ball first and finally, at this late stage in the game, the English team had created a one-on-one situation. Cassie dipped her left shoulder but allowed the ball to run across her body controlling it deftly with her right foot. Off balance, the centre back made a desperate lunge to make any kind of contact with ball or player, anything to prevent this danger which was now all too apparent. But Cassie was too slick, too nippy for the lumbering American. She was through on goal as the whole stadium and world television audience held its breath: so much depended on the next few seconds. Could the young English girl keep her cool in the face of what beckoned? Glory or failure, hero or one of history's little regarded footnotes, Cassie was about to decide her own destiny.

The American goalkeeper had realised the danger early. As soon as Cassie skipped past the last defender, she had raced from the goal line to narrow the available angle for Cassie to shoot at; she spread her arms, making herself look as big as possible. Surely there was no way Cassie could defeat such an imposing figure? But Cassie's touch had been good, the ball was running well for her, it wasn't stuck under her foot nor was it gathering pace away from her allowing the keeper to come out and smother the opportunity. Cassie glanced up; she knew precisely where and how she could score. There was a gap high to the keeper's right, she could power the ball into that top corner of the net and she shaped her body accordingly, left shoulder turned towards the all-important gap in the keeper's defences and her right leg drawn back for the necessary power. Now, Cassie, now! It was the moment for decisive action. But for a split-second Cassie stopped, a cunning feint allowing the keeper, who thought she had read Cassie's intentions, to sprawl to her right to close the apparent gap. Cassie had offered a dummy and the American keeper had snapped it up. Totally committed and sprawling to her right, the whole of the goal now lay undefended and with audacious nerve, Cassie rolled the ball over the goal line where it first rustled and then settled into the net. It was a combination of skill and momentous drama which silenced the whole stadium with both factions in the crowd not quite believing what they had just seen with their own eyes. Then it was a cue for pandemonium.

From where did Cassie get this additional energy? It was no longer a problem as she ran across to the corner flag and slid across the glossy green surface on her knees saluting a delirious section of the crowd and before long, she was engulfed by her joyous team mates and what seemed like the whole of England piled on top of her. Ca – ssie, Ca – ssie, Ca – ssie!

Turning from the monitor Cassie couldn't resist the broad grin of triumph as she faced more questions.

"Well, I've a feeling we'll be showing that particular clip for some time to come. The greatest occasion in women's football graced by one of the greatest goals ever scored." The interviewer directed one last question at Cassie. "How do you plan to celebrate tonight?"

As if scoring the winning goal for England in the World Cup Final was not already sufficient, in that moment, Cassie's answer endeared her to millions,

"Oh, I think I'll find somewhere quiet for a nice cup of tea."

## Chapter Fourteen

# Cats and the Crimea

Cassie looked around at her bedroom. Above her bed the posters remained in place. All of her favourite players and teams parading and posing with fixed grin smiles: all of them unaware of the drama in which Cassie had been involved. Her status as decisive goal scorer and World Cup Winner counted for nothing as she made the familiar transition to normal from fantasy. Alison was due to call any minute and they'd be able to compare notes about the final pulsating minutes of the match. Or rather they wouldn't, as far from showing any cognition that she herself had also featured in the match and had indeed picked up a World Cup Winner's medal at the end, Alison was showing growing irritation with Cassie's fantasies. Cassie fantasised and then all too often she caught Alison hoisting a polite smile in response. The message was becoming clear: adventures, escapades, derring-do and sporting heroics were becoming monotonous.

Apart from the football posters there had been some big changes in Cassie's bedroom. She'd pushed the bed as far into the corner as possible to make space for the cat display. Cassie and Alison's latest project was to make a film: Cat People, the Artist at Work. The digital camcorder had been set up on a tripod and Cassie was going to be filmed completing a cat drawing. Around her there were examples of completed pictures and work in progress. On the voice-over Alison was going to read from the poetry of Christopher Smart and T.S. Eliot. It was a brilliant idea and in order to prevent it from becoming too twee or domestic, Alison would also read from D.H. Lawrence's, Mountain Lion.

"And I think in this empty world there was room for me

And a mountain lion

And I think in the world beyond, how easily we might

Spare a million or two humans

And never miss them."

It was what Miss Jenkins was always saying to them, "Challenge your audience, make them think." So, what would they think? Was it possible to measure the value of human life against the life of an animal? *Men, the only animals in the world to fear.*

"Let's say six million humans." Alison had said, "It will have greater resonance." But the significance was lost on Cassie.

"Cassie!" Her mum was shouting from the bottom of the stairs. "Cassie!"

Cassie flung open the bedroom door, expecting the call to signify Alison's arrival. "Yes?"

"Your father's on the phone."

Cassie had often reflected on how her mum used the words father and dad; father to reflect a rather formal disapproval and dad to indicate a warmer response. The two moods varied and Cassie was fine-tuned for picking up nuances and mood indicators. She herself was still in a state of dull incomprehension about her dad's absence from the house. The day dad had said he was moving out still scorched on Cassie's memory.

"Are you too big to sit on your dad's knee?"

"I'm okay here, thank you."

Cassie sat resolutely at the end of the sofa. She knew; she just knew that something was wrong. Dad was obviously trying to look relaxed but all of his pet names for her jarred more awkwardly than ever. She kept telling him that she was too grown up for those names and now she felt the moment arriving when she was going to have to show how grown up she could be.

"You'll always be my own special girl; you know that don't you?"

No wonder dad worked in sales. He always had a winning way about him with his shiny dark hair and his kindly twinkly eyes and even now, at this terrible moment, Cassie desperately wanted to be his special girl. What could ever happen to prevent that? But she had to insist,

"I'm fourteen now and all that stuff has to stop."

Without acknowledging this dad pressed on,

"Your mum and I haven't been getting along too well."

Nothing new there. Cassie had tried to ignore the frequent arguments, or even worse, the terse exchanges and frosty silences. Yes, she knew, but wasn't it like a falling out at school? Weren't you supposed to make it all up and forget about whatever it was?

"We think it might be better if we give ourselves a bit of space."

Adults have this strange way of talking sometimes. "A bit of space." What on earth did that mean?

"We think you might benefit too. It can't be nice living in the middle of an argument."

Then don't argue. Stop it! Cassie wanted to drop all ideas about being grown up and scream at her father.

"So, I've got a little flat in town. It's not a penthouse by a long chalk, but it's cosy enough. You'll have to come and see it; I think you'll like it."

Cassie looked blankly at this man at the other end of the sofa who was still holding his reassuring smile.

"Where? Where is this flat?"

"It's in St Patrick's. Not far from the new Aldi."

So that's what a "bit of space" means: a flat in St Patrick's not far from the new Aldi.

"Come on, give me a hug. It doesn't mean that I've stopped loving you."

He beckoned her to shuffle along the sofa towards him.

"It doesn't mean I've stopped loving you." The words had made no sense; dad's moving out could only mean that he *had* stopped loving her.

Cassie took the phone from her mother. "Dad!"

"Hello, Princess."

"Dad, stop it! Don't call me that."

"Well, you are my Princess. Princess, Precious, my tiny Pixie." He was in a good mood; teasing.

"Dad, stop it or I'll put the phone down."

"Okay, I'm sorry. Listen, I've spoken to your mum and she's invited me for tea tonight. That okay?"

Cassie beamed. "Of course, it's okay. I'll make one of my special spag bols."

"That's what I was hoping you would say. About six o'clock?"

Cassie thought about the display of her work upstairs, the DVD: Cat People which ought to be ready by then. "Come earlier than that dad and I'll show you the project I'm working on with Ali."

"That would be nice love, but I'm working. I'm in Nottingham and I've got two calls to make in Sheffield. But God willing and a clear M1 and I'll see you at six. Okay?"

"Okay, Dad."

"Ciaou, Princess."

Mum took the receiver back and Cassie skipped upstairs to make last minute alterations to the display but paused long enough on the top landing to hear the last of the phone conversation from below.

"If you promised her six o'clock, make sure you are here at six."

So, the old argument was never far away: Dad's unreliability, his inability to keep his word, his constant making of grand plans which never reach fruition. Cassie could only hear one side of the conversation but she was quite sure that dad would be talking about his ambition and how he was working to benefit them all. Maybe that was right thought Cassie, maybe, but she couldn't see what benefit was gained by having Dad live in a shabby flat in town.

Realising how undignified it was to be eavesdropping on someone else's conversation Cassie stepped back into her bedroom. Everything was set and ready to go. She'd take one more look through the viewfinder just to be sure, not expecting in the slightest the shock she received.

"Oh!"

"Sorry Ma'am, did I startle you?"

It took a while for Cassie to gather herself. In fact, it took everything in her power not to scream out loud.

"Just a little bit. Who…" she couldn't find a polite way of asking this question, "Who are you?"

The tall, dark-haired person rose from the chair, stood to attention and saluted smartly. "Private William Bell, Ma'am." Then flustered he began to fumble with the top button of his tunic.

"What are you doing?" Cassie asked.

"Sorry Ma'am. I'd forgotten my top button was undone. Sloppy dress. My sergeant-major would have me on a charge for this."

"Look, don't worry about that." Cassie had gathered herself now and she wanted her unexpected guest to relax but he continued to fuss about his appearance as though he was reporting for duty. She decided that a more authoritative voice was needed.

"Right! At ease!"

To Cassie's alarm he stamped his left foot down, slightly apart from his right and then clapped his hands behind his back; still stiff, still formal, still awaiting inspection. Now it was Cassie's turn to be flustered, "No, what I mean is relax. You're off duty now. Take a seat."

"Well, if you're sure Ma'am."

He sat down still looking expectantly towards Cassie while Cassie looked straight back at this handsome boy soldier in his smart uniform. Okay, his pants were rather baggy; the bottoms rested on the top of his boots even though he was sitting down but it was his tunic which stole the show; the scarlet jacket with the gold braid fastenings across his chest and the proud epaulettes. His eyes shone, his face was bright and eager while his black hair was pushed carelessly off his forehead. With a shock Cassie realised that he wasn't much older than she was.

"You're a soldier?" She said rather stupidly.

"Yes, Ma'am. Private William Bell of the 17$^{th}$."

"You don't have to keep calling me Ma'am. Do you think you could call me Cassie?"

"Cassie?" He sounded uncertain.

"Yes, it's short for Cassandra. But I only get called that on Sundays and when I'm in trouble." Cassie's weak attempt at a joke failed. Private William Bell looked at her uncomprehendingly, so she continued, "Do you know what this is? She said pointing to the camcorder. It's a type of camera." She assumed he wouldn't know.

"I've seen a camera. Not like that one though. Mr Fenton brought a camera to the Crimea. Much bigger than that though; he brought his on a wagon."

"You've had your picture taken?"

"Yes, Miss. Mr Fenton took our images and said they might appear in the Times of London."

He'd settled for calling her Miss, and Cassie realised that she would probably have to settle for that too.

"Well William, I'm going to take your photograph too, but you don't have to remain still with this camera, you can move around and talk. You can tell me all about yourself. Okay?"

"That would be fine, Miss. And begging your pardon, do you think you could call me Will?"

"Will?" For a moment, Cassie was caught in a moment of startled recognition but then she composed herself again. "I'm sure I could, Will." Cassie pressed the button for record. "You say you've been to the Crimea. What can you tell me about that? At least Cassie felt she could take control of this conversation; didn't she know all about the Crimea? Hadn't she done a great project on Florence Nightingale? And Will wanted to talk; he was totally unfazed by this strange looking silver box on a tripod.

"We were a proud sight, Miss. Hundreds of us: the seventeenth regiment, the eighty-eighth, the fifth Dragoon Guards, the Forty Second Royal Highland regiment and the Seventy First Highland regiment all in their tartan finery. The horses, the cannons and all the tents pitched in straight lines as far as the eye could see. The good Queen herself would have been proud to see us all there, Miss."

"You were fighting for the Queen?"

"The Queen, Country and Empire, Miss. doing our duty."

"But you were at Balaklava."

"Yes, Miss."

"What happened there?"

"We did our duty, Miss. We fought for Queen and Country. But more than that, I can't say. There are some things that aren't suitable for a lady's ears."

Cassie bridled at the perceived need for protection. "But you left your family and friends to go and fight at Balaklava? Didn't you have any regrets?"

Will paused. "Oh, I had regrets alright. I'd spent my days on a farm. I'd grown up around horses. I knew horses. I could talk to them and they would understand. I would have liked to be in a cavalry regiment. In a different life I would have had the money for a rank in the cavalry. They looked ever so proud trotting to the front. And then so many horses, dead and wounded. Terrible, Miss. They didn't deserve that."

"Nor did you." Cassie wanted to shout at this boy who was so hung up with duty and fighting for the Queen. "What did it achieve?"

"We did our duty, Miss."

But didn't he have a duty to his family? Didn't he have a duty to care for the horses on the farm? What was the point in being blown apart on a Crimean battlefield? Cassie turned to switch off the camcorder and then turned back to face Will, but he had gone. All that was left was the parade of cat pictures with each cat gazing inscrutably back at Cassie.

## Chapter Fifteen

# A Kickabout in the Park

Once again Cassie looked out of her bedroom window to the houses on the opposite side of the road and beyond that to another set of roofs and another set beyond that. So many roofs, satellite dishes well-kept gardens, fronts turned over to gravel or paving. In each of these houses, televisions were blaring, children were crying, homework was being done, meals were being prepared, babies were being made and visitors were eagerly sought by the lonely. How many people lived within Cassie's wandering gaze now? Fifty thousand? A full house at United? Double that for a hundred thousand, then multiply that by ten. Was that a million? The arithmetic was getting too much for Cassie. A million then, and multiply that by six. Her head was about to explode with attempting to cope with these figures. Six million people. How many crying voices, homeworks, dinners and copulations did that represent? What did Alison mean by six million people would have a greater resonance?

And what of Will? She knew with absolute certainty that she had met him before, and she knew with equal certainty that if she set the camcorder to playback there would be nothing there. Will was real, he had spoken to her, he had been awkward and uneasy about his uniform and how he should address her, but he had also been passionate about the plight of the horses in battle and adamant about doing his duty. Fight, kill and die, he had been absolutely unbending about it. *He* may have been brought up on a farm, *he* may have been good with horses, but a lot of his soldier colleagues would have been from the burgeoning big cities of the growing Empire, the smog-bound rat infested, over-crowded hovels which serviced Britain's industrial might. His colleagues would have signed up to escape the poverty of the slums, the workhouse and prison. Florence Nightingale may have made a name for herself but the women who had worked for her returned to England to find that their names were besmirched; treating wounded and dying men had left them little better than prostitutes. "Challenge your reader," Miss Jenkins had said, but Cassie now found that she was challenging herself. The Empire had been built on the lives of lads like Will who went to places they couldn't even pick out on a map; fight, kill and die.

"Cassie!" Mum again, calling from downstairs. "Phone call," she added resignedly. Cassie trotted down to take the receiver. "Will that be all madam? May I take the rest of the day off?" Mum was in a sarky mood.

"Shhh!" said Cassie irritated before speaking into the phone. "Hi!"

"Hi, Cassie!" A boy's voice; Simon, Alison's older brother. "Bad news from little Sis I'm afraid. She's got some kind of lurgy thing. She's throwing up for England so I don't think she'll be coming round to yours."

"Lurgy? Should I pop round and see her?"

"I wouldn't if I were you." Simon laughed, "It's probably deadly contagious and anyway, when she's not yelling for Hughie in the bathroom she retreats to her bed and falls unconscious under two duvets."

Mum was picking up half of the conversation and looking concerned. Cassie turned away from her towards the wall in a vain attempt to gain some privacy.

"We were going to make a film this afternoon."

"I know you were," Simon continued, "But if your plans are off, why not join us? Craig from next door fancies a kickabout in the park; just one on one and a goalkeeper. What about it?"

Cassie quickly took stock of the changed circumstances of the afternoon. One plan disappears, another one turns up out of the blue. "Yeah, sure. Give me ten minutes and I'll meet you there."

"Great!" Simon's enthusiasm bounced down the phone line. "Oh, and Cassie, bring your football, eh?"

Cassie replaced the phone. Her mum hadn't moved, she was waiting for a full resume of the call. Cassie knew she had no option if she wanted a quiet life.

"Ali's ill: some kind of deadly lurgy apparently. She's in bed fast asleep so there's no point in taking her a bunch of grapes. Simon and Craig fancy a kickabout in the park so I'm going to meet them."

Mum smiled, "Simon. Now there's a young man who meets with my full approval."

"Muuum!" Cassie stretched out the single syllable as far as she could, "They only want me to play because I've got a decent football."

"That's boys for you," still smiling, Mum had a twinkle in her eye, "Only after one thing, eh?"

Completely exasperated, Cassie went to dig out a pair of trainers.

* * * * *

One versus one can be absolutely exhausting, so the thing to do is to play in the continental manner, like the Italian league Cassie sometimes watched: slow, slow, slow and then a sudden burst of energy when an opportunity arose. Possession of the ball was vital as any carelessness with it could give your opponent a clear run in to goal. And against these lads Cassie knew she would always come off second best in any sustained physical challenge for the ball. She knew she had to play to her strengths, using her nippiness and ability to change direction quickly to her advantage. Look at Simon for instance: big, solid and effective in defending in front of goal. What she had to do was to lure him away from the goalmouth, give herself a chance to make him over-commit and exploit any space he left behind himself.

This was exactly how things were shaping up. Giving every impression of being worn out, Cassie was toying with the ball, looking as though she lacked the energy to keep it under control. Simon was being lured further and further from the goal sensing that soon there would be an opportunity to take advantage. Cassie waited and waited, any second now she was ready to make the dramatic spurt and just as Simon was about to poke out a tentative leg, she had her chance. Now! Cassie's speed took Simon completely by surprise. She dipped her left shoulder forcing Simon to adjust his balance and he completely over-compensated, throwing his body in one direction while Cassie smartly took the ball in the opposite. Hopelessly out of position now, Simon turned and desperately tried to make up the vital lost metres as Cassie bore down on Craig in the makeshift park goals.

Craig was confident; he had little doubt that he could intimidate this attacker with his superior size and positioning sense. Besides, she had glanced to his right-hand side and betrayed her intentions. Craig flung himself to his right as Cassie prepared to shoot. But the dive was aimed at thin air as Cassie sold him the dummy and then simply rolled the ball into the vacant goal.

It should have been her moment of triumph: a defender beaten by skill and a goalkeeper hopelessly fooled in the build up to a goal of consummate skill, a goal good enough to win the World Cup final. But Simon, who wasn't one to give up any cause as lost, had been charging back to defend the goal; last ditch tackles were a specialty of his, only this time he was too late, the ball had gone and his tackle was a futile foul. He barged into Cassie and as she toppled, he fell on top of her and felt the sudden expulsion of air from her body as he sandwiched her to the ground.

That he was playing against a young girl was now all too apparent to Simon. Not only younger, but she was also smaller and softer and as he disentangled his long legs from the gasping body, he realised he should have shown some restraint, he should have demonstrated a little chivalrous reserve in his commitment.

"Are you alright?" Simon sat up and tentatively touched Cassie on the elbow. His question was redundant as his opponent, badly winded, was trying to gulp in lungfuls of air. She slowly climbed to her feet and doubled up again to try and regain normal breathing. She gave Simon a short wave of her hand. Sure, she was fine, just unable to breathe or talk normally for a moment. And then slowly, in the face of Simon's agonised concern, Cassie's expression changed from agony to pleasure and with impish delight she finally announced,

"Goal to me, and a six-three lead."

Craig, who had managed to avoid the physical pile- up, was equally relieved and impressed. "How did you do that, Cassie? I mean I thought I had everything covered." He added sheepishly, "You sent me in completely the wrong direction. It was like you had been practising that for ages."

Cassie laughed, "If I told you how I learned that move, you would never believe me."

No harm done then. A sunny day in the park, the early days of the summer holidays and three friends taking a breather and the chance to take pleasure in each other's abilities.

If they hadn't been so engaged in their exploits, they might have seen the three boys who were crossing the park, slouching in their direction. They might have seen the boys and picked up something about their manner and mood. The two taller boys moved with a sullen, shoulders-hunched lurch. The third boy, slightly smaller and maybe younger, had a cockier gait. All three wore a uniform of hooded grey sweat tops, and all three had seen the footballers and in an unspoken communication had agreed upon their potential as a target.

After Cassie's goal, the ball had rolled beyond their folded tops which formed the temporary goalposts. It was the smallest of the three newcomers who picked it up and walked cheekily with it placed on the flat of his hand.

"Whose is this crappy ball?"

For the first time, Simon, Cassie and Craig turned and began to take stock of the newcomers; began to gauge the incipient hostility.

"I said, whose crappy ball?"

Simon stepped forward, "It's mine." At which point, with an ugly punt, the boy kicked the ball as far as he could across the park.

Simon's response was an involuntary, "You pillock!" Which was all the excuse the boy needed: a critical response, a hostile attitude, however minor, was sufficient. He had been provoked and this was more than enough justification for the punch which he lanced out at Simon's mouth meeting its target with a sickening smack. Stung, Simon staggered back a couple of paces to maintain his balance and the boy watched him keenly. Would Simon respond to the punch? He was ready for him if he did and his two mates could watch and be impressed. But Simon wouldn't fight back, nor would Craig; some atavistic rule had been asserted and they didn't have the desire or the malign impulse to challenge it. The tension eased as the three grey-clad boys realised they had reinforced their position. It was only Cassie whose outrage had yet to be expressed.

"You pig!" she yelled at Simon's assailant.

The boy looked at her dismissively. "Shut up, you. Concentrate on your football." And his face morphed into an ugly leer. "Don't these get in the way when you dribble?" And he made a grab at Cassie's breasts.

"Fuck off!"

The boys jeered and set off across the park.

"Get your girlfriend to do your fighting," one of the boys called as they continued their journey satisfied with the violent interlude.

The mood was killed and no further play was entertained. For Simon and Craig, it had been a shaming experience; their notions of their own manhood had taken a battering. Craig fetched Cassie's football and the three of them walked home thoroughly subdued. Craig went straight in but Cassie insisted that Simon should let her mum have a look at the ugly swelling which was forming around his mouth. Simon wasn't keen but Cassie's mum had a nursing background and if he let her deal with his injuries, it might save a bit of fuss when he got home.

Cassie's Mum's first response was to make a joke when she saw the early return of the footballers but she soon changed her tack when she picked up the grim mood.

"What have you done to yourself?" She said to Simon as she put her fingers under his chin and lifted his mouth up to the light.

"A goalmouth collision in the football," answered Simon. Cassie's mum looked at him doubtfully.

"It wasn't, Mum." Cassie did not want to enter into any pretence and she retold the whole story as Simon had a small trace of blood cleaned from the corner of his mouth where the skin was broken.

"Teeth okay, Simon? Anything loose?" Cassie's mum was ultra efficient knowing that a more kindly, comforting approach would further damage Simon's self-respect. "Did you know those lads? You should tell the police."

Simon refused. As far as he was concerned the whole incident was best regarded as being over now. It wasn't how it should have been. Right was clearly on their side: his, Craig's and Cassie's, and by rights he should have given those lads a good hiding. It's how it works in films; honour is satisfied and a moral balance is maintained. But no, he wouldn't be telling the police.

"Well, if that's how you feel Simon, there's only one thing you can do now..." Cassie's mum had finished her ministrations. There'd be a swollen lip for a while, a bit of bruising, but certainly no long-term physical damage.

"What's that?"

"You can stay with us and have a nice cup of tea."

## Chapter Sixteen

# Sealed with a Kiss

Dear Mum,

If you are reading this then the worst has happened. There's no point in pretending that it couldn't when we all knew otherwise. We've had this conversation too often to go over it again; we are soldiers who signed up to go and fight and people die as a result of fighting. I chose to sign up and I chose to accept the possible consequences.

That doesn't make this letter any easier to write of course. It's part of our pre-tour ritual: we write our last letter and hope it's no such thing, we give a DNA sample for foolproof identification and we have out photograph taken. Morbidly, this is called the Death Photograph. We are encouraged not to grin too widely but to aim for a more military pose; to capture the qualities of valour and honour for the press and the tele, and we know how and when it's likely to be used. You don't want someone making rabbit's ears behind you on a photograph like that, do you? But of course, everyone laughs about these things. It's our coping strategy, knowing the reality of what we do is never too far removed.

And it's that reality I want to touch upon now. I know you've argued with me about this but let me say that I truly believe in what I am doing, in what the army and the country is doing. We face a threat to our way of life and to the traditions we hold so dearly: the democratic process, the respect for other religious traditions and equality for women. I think this way because this is the way I've been brought up by you and dad. (There's also a letter addressed to him by the way.) You always spoke about fairness and tolerance, you always cared deeply about our responsibilities to others because when all was said and done, we were much better off than other people; we were privileged.

Now I consider it a privilege to serve as a soldier in this beautiful horrific country and it is something I do proudly: proud of my colleagues, proud of the cause and proud of my family background. And these are the really difficult words to write because I have never spoken them, I have never told you to your face but I am determined to let you know that I appreciate how much you've done for me, both of you. You are both bitterly opposed to this war, and Dad still has a problem with women in the army, doesn't he? And yet I know you support my decision fully and that gives me incredible strength. I love you both deeply and it is my sincerest hope that you don't find that out through reading this letter. But if you do, accept these words and the simple sincerity in which they are offered. Don't cry any tears for me as I've done what I consider to be the right thing to do and I've done it in the service of my country and in the unshakeable security of your love. If you can, don't be angry but try to be proud of me. I am what I am, I am doing my duty.

But now I must sign off. A table tennis challenge has been issued and, you know me, winning is everything and besides, there are drinks at stake.

Yours always,

Lieutenant Cassandra Jackson

(Cassie)

## Chapter Seventeen

# Tending to the Sick and Needy

Simon showed Cassie in. Awkwardness hung in the air like a stale smell impossible to shift.

"How are you?"

"I'm fine." Simon managed a smile. "It's not me you've come to see though, is it?"

Looking at Simon wasn't usually a problem but Cassie tried not to look too closely at the bruising on his face.

"No, it's Ali. How is she?"

"See for yourself. She's sitting like the Queen of Sheba in the front room. Go on through."

Cassie, knowing her way round Alison's house, didn't need any directions. She pushed open the door into the lounge and saw Alison sitting in a dressing gown snugly perched on the sofa with her feet tucked beneath her. Her hair had been neatly brushed but her face retained the white pallor of the recently ill. This wasn't the Alison that Cassie knew, Ali who was always in tip-top form, who always projected perfection.

"Wow, you look ghastly!"

"Thanks, you've made me feel better already."

Cassie laughed. "I'm sorry, it wasn't meant to sound like that. What I meant was I've seen you look better."

"Yeah well, I've just beaten the world record for throwing up over the last few days."

"So, I hear." Cassie managed a more sympathetic tone. "How are you feeling now? How's your appetite? I haven't brought you any grapes, but I've got this." She proffered a package wrapped in silver foil to her friend.

"What is it?"

"Lemon drizzle cake; made by my own fair hand. Well, with a bit of help from mum. We've been busy."

"I can see." Alison took the package. "You're a girl of many talents: artist, footballer, cake maker. You don't really need your flights of fancy, do you?"

The comment passed like a flash of kingfisher blue and before Cassie could take on board the implications, Alison let out a shout of surprising volume for one so frail.

"Simon!"

Dutifully, Simon appeared at the door and he received his instructions.

"Be a pet and pop this in the kitchen. We might try a piece later with a cup of tea. Thank you, Bro."

Alison smiled sweetly while Simon did his best not to scowl.

"I'll be glad when you're fit and well again." He muttered, taking the cake and leaving the room.

"Such a sweetie." Alison turned to Cassie, "But what's all this about him brawling in the park like a common hooligan?"

Cassie didn't share the joke. "It wasn't funny, Ali, those boys were pigs. They should be sorted out."

"How do you mean?"

"Well, they shouldn't be allowed to go around like that, hitting people for no reason." Some of Cassie's outrage resurfaced. "What has Simon said about it?"

"Not much. In fact, less than that, nothing. You know what boys are like, a fight sorts everything out. Shows who's the biggest dog in the pack."

"It wasn't a fight," Cassie protested. "It was an unprovoked attack."

"Yeah, and Simon didn't fight back and lost his self-respect big time. He won't want to talk about that."

Cassie thought back to how well Simon had carried himself, refusing to lower himself to their level.

"That's crazy. I'd like to see those boys get some of their own medicine."

It was Alison's turn to respond. "Are you going to go round and thump them? Or are you going to get a bigger gang than theirs to beat them up? That makes you just as bad as them, doesn't it?"

Cassie struggled with an issue she hadn't really thought through. Her sense of injustice burned fiercely, and had done since their kick-about in the park had been so abruptly ended. Her sense of fair play had been offended. Where was the justice?

"No, I don't mean that. I just think that the people who are right should be protected."

"I don't get you."

Alison was struggling with the whole discussion. She had been pleased to see her friend, but she hadn't expected to wrestle with the complexities of right and wrong and whether or not the use of force was ever justified.

Cassie made a last attempt to explain herself. "Okay, there'll always be fighting of some sort, right? So, we should make sure that the people who are decent, who want to get on with their lives without any bother, should be allowed to do so. If they are attacked, they should know that there will be a force to protect them."

"Wow, get you!" Alison laughed. "Wonder Woman, ready to change in a telephone kiosk and save the world at a moment's notice. I'll tell you what, before you go on a crusade, should we put the kettle on and see if I can keep any of that cake down?"

It was a better plan than trying to keep world order, and besides, there was something that Alison had wanted to say to Cassie for some time now. A glint came into her eyes. "Cassie, I think you fancy my brother."

Cassie's denial was too immediate and too strong.

"No, I don't."

"Imagine that! Cassie and my big, useless lump of a brother."

Again, Cassie was far too strenuous in her defence.

"He's not a big, useless lump."

"Ah! So, you do fancy him."

"No, I don't," said Cassie, tantalised by this turn in the conversation. "You're worse than my mum."

"Why? Does she fancy him as well?"

It was a welcome diversion, taking the heat off Cassie. Both girls snorted laughter and began to speculate.

"If they got married, you'd be my aunty."

"You would be my favourite niece." Alison wiped her eye. This was better than lying ill in bed. "Come on, let's put that kettle on."

But before the conversation evaporated completely and the tingle began to fade, Cassie added, "He *is* quite nice though, your Simon."

In the event, Alison tried only a small piece of cake with her cup of tea but there were no ill effects. They talked, they laughed, they watched their favourite DVDs and by the end of the afternoon they had slipped into that comfortable niche of friendship – like pulling on an old, baggy sweatshirt. Alison was tired but cheered by her friend's visit while Cassie was pleased to be the stronger one for once, pleased that Alison had to depend on her for some minor fetching and carrying. So pleased that she almost forgot about the horrid event in the park, almost forgot that on the same day, Dad had rung up from some motorway service station to say that he was delayed at work and wouldn't be able to make it for tea after all.

## Chapter Eighteen

# Dream Lover

In the end Cassie chose her black top. It was simple but smart, casual but with just the right level of elegance. In fact, she had probably known all along that she would pick out that top eventually, but the choosing had been fun. The preparation too was part of a lengthy, pleasurable ritual: showering, shampooing and conditioning, dusting herself in a dusky talc, wrapping herself in a big, fluffy bathrobe while expertly applying light, subtle make-up. She chose her best black trousers to go with the top and her classiest shoes with just the suggestion of a heel; this wouldn't be an evening for tottering about and risking a broken ankle. The final touch was to apply glitter for some sparkle before she stood before the full-length mirror for an appraisal. Perfect: sophisticated and a shade enigmatic. Now, just a dab of perfume and she became sophisticated, enigmatic and sexy.

There was a light knock on the bedroom door. Mum would normally bellow up the stairs but tonight she chose to pop her head round the door and announce proudly, "Simon's here."

Cassie did her best to glide into the downstairs reception room and Simon stood up to meet her. He too was dressed very smartly: black suit and white shirt with a silk tie left insouciantly askew. Smart? He looked devastating, especially when he smiled at Cassie and left his eyes lingering.

"Well, off you go, you two. Don't forget that after midnight everything returns to normal and it'll be all pumpkins and mice." Mum ushered them to the door.

Simon was the perfect gentleman, holding the passenger door for Cassie as she slipped into the plush saloon. He got in on the driver's side and brushed aside Cassie's complimentary comments about the car.

"It gets me from A to B."

But they sailed regally through the city streets with just a hum from under the bonnet and the occasional weighty tock tock from the indicators. At ease with the leather upholstery and air of deep comfort, Simon drove with assurance, every manoeuvre exuded confidence and his conversation put Cassie into relax mode. He asked her politely about her day and listened attentively to what Cassie could only think were humdrum details of her life.

"I nearly forgot to feed the cat."

"Well, I'm glad you remembered. It wouldn't do to return home to an angry Coco demanding some dinner."

When had she told him the cat's name was Coco?

Simon turned into the floodlit drive of a hotel pulling up by the impressive front door where a footman stepped out and Simon casually tossed him the keys for parking. It was grand, very grand and not a little bit overwhelming.

"Here, take my arm." It was almost as if Simon knew. Gratefully, Cassie was led into a high-ceilinged reception room where it seemed as though everyone knew Simon and wanted to make polite conversation with him. She was introduced as Cassandra and she noticed that she too was warmly accepted into Simon's social circle. Any friend of Simon's…it seemed.

"Your table is ready for you, Mr Jones."

They were led through the dining room to a table for two. Simon waited until Cassie took her place and then he too sat down.

"It was really rather unfair of me to bring you here tonight."

Cassie was startled. She was just beginning to think how wonderful it all was: the thick carpets, the beautifully laid tables, chandeliers that sparkled overhead.

"Unfair. Why?"

"Because all of the other ladies will feel most put out to be so outshone."

"You're an outrageous flatterer," she told him, secretly thrilled.

"I speak only the truth." He returned her smile and noticed how her eyes shone in the candlelight. "Later, we'll dance, but before that we'll eat. But first, let's order some champagne."

So, Cassie Jackson, the elegantly dressed in black sophisticate, began her dream date by laughing and spluttering with champagne bubbles up her nose.

It *was* late when she was safely escorted home but her outfit didn't turn to rags, nor had Simon's car transformed into a pumpkin. Instead, she sat at her dressing table and mentally ticked off all of the wonderful moments. How courteous Simon had been throughout, how being Simon's date had ensured that she was the centre of attention, how he'd put her at her ease in the face of an intimidating menu and chosen appropriate wines without any fuss. And then the dancing, how he'd glided her across the floor with a strong supporting hand in the small of her back while he sang softly into her ear along to the band's music, his voice warm and mellow, crooning about how lovely she looked tonight.

And when it seemed as though their legs were finally giving up and they couldn't dance any more, he'd suggested a breath of fresh air on the terrace and they'd stepped out into the cool of the evening and walked a little and talked a little and then kissed: a glorious kiss under the dreamlike night sky and the millions of twinkling, sparkling stars.

## Chapter Nineteen

# All Hands to the Deck

It seemed as though summer was finally going to arrive. From early morning the sun had been glinting on the bottom of the Jackson's garden highlighting the old wooden shed and the sprawling peony bushes, moving higher into the sky and turning its attention to the back of the house. The grey patchy sky had slowly given way to a blue deep enough to dive into. The morning was rolling up its sleeves; it was time for action, time to show what a summer's day was all about. It was going to be hot, although hopefully, not too hot as Mrs Jackson had plans: the decking and the conservatory badly needed a coat of wood stain. It was a job which had been put off for a year now, maybe more. It didn't do to reckon up too closely.

Cassie had volunteered to help and she even turned down the chance of a late reprieve.

"Wouldn't you prefer to go round to see Alison?"

"No, she's still confined to the house. I'd rather be out and about."

"That's the spirit." Her mum was pleased. "We'll soon have this job cracked. We'll form a women's partnership."

All of the necessary gear had been assembled: dust sheets, wire wool, masking tape, tins of varnish, brushes of various sizes and a bucket of soapy water had been brought round ready for the washing down of the woodwork.

"You've got this all organised, haven't you, Mum?" Cassie was impressed.

"That's the idea. Organisation and planning are the key to any successful campaign."

Cassie wiped her hands down the old pair of jeans she'd chosen for her day of labouring. "I mean you're not put out at having to do a man's job?"

Her mum looked at her with exaggerated shock and horror.

"Well! I never thought I'd see the day when a daughter of mine said such a thing!" But she was laughing. "We women fought that battle a long time ago. Now go and clean out your mouth with soapy water, or else make a start on washing down this woodwork."

Cassie picked a wet sponge out of the bucket and applied it to the window frame on the conservatory. Immediately a line of water ran down her wrist and outstretched arm beneath her cotton shirt sleeve. She stopped to roll up her sleeves and thought: *I didn't mean that about a man's job, I meant it was a job really for Dad.*

Progress had been quick. It hadn't taken long to wash down the woodwork despite the number of spiders' webs they encountered. Cassie had gritted her teeth as spiders darted from hidden corners as soon as their web was touched. She washed them all away as this was no time for being girly. And in no time at all the woodwork was washed down and it was drying nicely in the warm sunshine. Now they could get on with the rubbing down, banishing flaking pieces of old varnish and preparing a surface for the new coat to come. This was harder work, more of a physical effort, but Cassie found it oddly satisfying. Between them they had worked and talked. It was odd how conversation was much easier when there was another job at hand.

"I knew we should have chosen a UPVC conservatory." Cassie's mum complained. "Much easier to maintain."

"Oh no, Mum. The wood is much nicer!"

"Just like your dad, you. He chose wood. Never mind the upkeep he said, think of the aesthetics. Aesthetics! I ask you: always with his head in the clouds."

Cassie stole a look at her mum. "Do you miss him, Mum? I mean, do you ever wish he was still here. Living here I mean?"

Bev Jackson was aware of the warm intimacy between mother and daughter which had been nurtured by the summer sunshine and the sense of comradeship in doing a physical task together. This was about more than simply sprucing up a conservatory, but she also knew it was still not time to own up to the long, lonely nights she'd endured, the nights of tears in a darkened bedroom.

"Of course, I do, love. And your dad can come back. He knows that. He's just got to get his head right."

"What's wrong with his head?"

"It's on a different planet. That's what's wrong with his head. He was always full of grand plans, your dad. At one time he was always talking about Australia, he thought Australia could provide the life he was looking for. That fell through and then we were going to start a luxury bed and breakfast in the Caribbean somewhere."

"That doesn't sound too bad. Where was it, Jamaica? Barbados?"

"Oh, love it doesn't matter where it was going to be, it was never going to happen. Then when the fantasy life style faded, he grew bitter about his lot, about promotions which didn't come his way and all he would do is make bigger and bigger plans, tilting at bigger and bigger windmills. Your dad is a dreamer and reality never matches up to his dreamworld ambitions."

Cassie continued scraping at the woodwork not daring to think what damage she was inflicting on her fingernails.

"You always encourage me to be ambitious."

"Yes, Love, but keep it real. Keep your ambitions rooted in the real world and remember what's important."

"What is important?"

"That's for you to decide." She smiled at her daughter who now had a dark wisp of hair across her face and a bead of sweat trickling down the bridge of her nose. "Your values; you sort that out for yourself."

It was a conversation stopper, a moment to think over what her mum had said as she'd attacked the next window frame with her piece of wire wool. She could do that; she could sort out what was important: friends for instance and being true to yourself. Then she stopped, alarmed at how quickly her thought processes had come to an end. Why wasn't she being true to herself? Why was the real Cassie Jackson being submerged? She could find no immediate answer; some mazes are just too complicated for finding a way out. She'd be better off working on the grime on the window frame.

Good progress was being made. Despite the growing heat the preparation was almost complete. Masking tape still needed to be applied to the edges of the window panes before the wood was stained but the two workers were able to stand back and admire the results of their efforts. That was the point when they were interrupted by a visitor whose knocking at the front door had not been heard so he had wandered around the back to find the great conservatory restoration project in progress. For once he looked a little uncertain of himself with his hands slumped into his pockets as adjusted his weight from foot to foot.

"Alison's still not allowed out." Simon felt as though some kind of explanation was necessary.

"I know," Cassie replied. "I texted her this morning."

"Oh, I just thought I would pop round and tell you."

"Did she say she wanted me to go and see her?"

"No, no, not at all. I think she's reading. She's stuck indoors, but you already know that." An uncomfortable pause; there was still plenty of work to be done and a visitor who was at a loose end. It was Simon who ended the silence.

"Could I stay?"

Cassie's mum turned to Simon. "That, young man is music to my ears, if it was an offer of help that is. We need someone with a bit of reach and you fit the bill perfectly. Someone up there must be listening to us. Besides, I'm going in now to put some biscuits in the oven and make the coffee. Cassie, can you show our new helper the ropes?"

Cassie thought about welcoming Simon to the women's partnership but then thought better of it. There weren't many ropes to show, they just had to apply some masking tapes to all of the window edges.

Perhaps it was easier said than done. Simon's reach *did* come in handy as he was able to hold the tape in position while Cassie cut it to a necessary length. There was some awkward stretching and squeezing though, sometimes when they were pushed into close proximity. Reaching up with the scissors Cassie was all too aware of the strong body right next to hers. She could feel his chest expand and contract with his breathing; he was slender and dishy, lots of girls at school fancied him and Cassie was in no hurry to complete the task. Simon Jones! He was also two years above her at school and he was Ali's brother. Did that make any difference? Ali was completely oblivious to Simon's charms; you don't even think of your brother in those terms. How would Ali feel about Simon and Cassie? Cassie and Simon? Cassie tried out the combinations in her head: Simon and Cassie, Cassie and Simon, Simon and Cassie.

"I'm going to get cramp if you don't cut that paper soon." Simon was holding his stretched position.

"Stop moaning, I've got to get this job right."

"It's masking tape," he told her, "You're not hanging the Mona Lisa."

"Who's Moaning Lisa?"

"Come on, get a move on."

"There! All done."

Simon stepped away and rubbed his back. "Thank goodness for that. What took you so long?"

"Perfectionism," smiled Cassie. "You don't rush an artist at work. Should we make a start on the staining or do you want to wait for Mum to bring out a drink?"

Simon sat down heavily on the garden wall making his answer clear enough.

"Is that all you came round for? To tell me that Ali is still stuck in the house?"

"No, I wanted to get involved in a house make-over. When's the tele crew coming round?"

"There'd better not be a tele crew coming round if I've got this old thing on." Cassie pulled at the old checked shirt which had been wet earlier that morning and now was just creased, fraying and unkempt.

"You look fine." Simon's compliment took her aback. At least she thought it was a compliment. Before she could think about it any further, he continued. "Have you got any free time at all?"

"Yeah, I suppose so."

"We could do something."

"Like what? You want another game of football?"

"No, we could hang about, see a film or something."

The words hung in the air: see a film? What a DVD or go to the cinema? if it was go to the cinema, beyond a "yeah" or a "sure", Cassie didn't know what to say apart from, "I'll have to ask and see" which she didn't say because even in her head it sounded particularly young and stupid. And then there was no chance to say anything at all because her mum appeared round the corner carrying a tray with a jug of squash and a pot of coffee.

“No biscuits yet, they’re not ready. Why has all the work stopped?”

It wasn’t just the work that had stopped; Cassie felt that her brain had gone into meltdown too. What did Simon want? To hang about? Just him and her? Had he really asked her for a date? The problem posed by a peeling conservatory now faded into insignificance and this new predicament couldn’t be solved with wire wool and a bucket of soapy water.

## Chapter Twenty

# Mad Dogs and Englishwomen

They warn you all about it; about the heat and dangers of dehydration, but no warning is enough. Even the most belting day in England is no preparation for the hot season in Afghanistan. No one can be fully prepared for the heat, the oppressive force which can drain the last fluid ounce out of a body, the crushing humidity. Nor can you be prepared for the dust which gets everywhere, the flies, the poverty, and sneakily, the appalling beauty of the place. At any other time, Cassie would have gazed beyond the compound across the Green Zone to where the mountains shimmered in the distance. What a beautiful land, and what dangers lay in the hundreds of miles stretched out before her.

"It's strangely beautiful, isn't it?" Cassie turned to Alison.

"Yes, there's a terrible beauty."

Cassie felt certain that Alison was quoting poetry again and neither of them could afford to let concentration slip, even when they weren't on patrol.

"What are we doing here, Ali?"

"You know the answer to that one." Alison joshed her friend, "We've all been well briefed on that."

Cassie swatted at an early bothersome fly. As the day wore on it would multiply, the flies weren't deterred by 40-degree heat.

"No, I know all that stuff: preserving our way of life, fighting terrorism, promoting democracy blah, blah, blah. But we're nearly 40,000 miles from home. It's got nothing to do with us. Why don't we just let them get on with it?"

Alison was concerned. A tour of duty in Afghanistan was more difficult than people could imagine. People at home in supermarkets and pubs only wanted to hear about the so-called glamour of fighting the Taliban. They only wanted to bandy about words like *courage* and *hero*. They didn't realise that a tour of Afghanistan could leave you vulnerable in so many ways: homesickness was one, losing the will to fight was another.

"Come on, Cassie. We shouldn't even be having this conversation, you know that." She tugged at her friend. "Up you get. Let's go to the gym and sweat it out."

Cassie pulled away from her friend's gentle grip. "No, Ali. I mean what are *we* doing here? Two birds amongst all of these blokes."

"Oh, not that one again. We're not just two birds. There's almost seven hundred birds in the British Army. You might say there's a whole flock of birds."

Cassie had to laugh at how Alison had picked up on the derogatory word. Typical Alison; she knew where problems and tensions lay but she always dealt with them professionally. Calm and serene; she was a swan, that was the kind of bird that Alison was. She felt safe alongside Alison as well, I mean, you don't go provoking swans, do you? And at least she hadn't replied with all that guff about women's rights in Afghan, promoting education and voting and so on. Because every time they went out on patrol on this women's rights crusade they returned to the base and tents that were festooned with pin ups of topless women. Cassie had once said, "We're fighting for their rights to have their tits photographed."

Alison had countered, "As far as you're concerned, you need to keep their respect. Be reliable, be part of the team, match them in the gym and they won't mind if you're a bird, a bloke or a performing monkey."

Cassie had to smile again. Alison continued, "Of course, it always helps if you can give them a damned good game of table tennis."

The compound lacked facilities. Conditions were cramped, there was little or no room for preserving delicate sensibilities, changing often took place publicly within tents with little fuss or comment. A modified shipping container served as a shower and one single latrine was reserved for women soldiers only and these were the only places where privacy could be maintained. But it was often a short-lived privacy, especially in the latrine as the flies were the ultimate power brokers. The quality of life was enhanced by the arrival of the Chinook, chopping its way across the arid landscape with a net of goodies slung below, positioning itself for landing like a giant hornet, sweeping up an angry cloud of dust. But it brought luxuries: food for the kitchens, drinks for the machines and the eagerly awaited post from home. Parcels were seized upon and torn open, letters were read, family triumphs were relayed loudly, toiletries were hoarded while jaffa cakes and hobnobs were generously dispensed. Bad news was very often folded and stashed away to be dealt with later.

Order always had to be maintained. Kit had to be kept immaculately, weapons checked thoroughly and fitness levels could be topped up on the running machines. And then there was the boredom: another enemy skulking around the camp. It could be fought off at the dart board or more often at the slightly wonky table tennis table.

"Okay! A round robin for the championship of Sangin, of Afghanistan, in fact the whole world." Dave Thomas made the announcement. He was probably the best player in the gun crew but he didn't make a big show of that or shout about it in any way. Life in Afghanistan taught you not to make yourself conspicuous, the priorities were making sure you did your job well, your mates would be relying on you and teamwork was everything. No-one wanted to make a target of their self, nor did anyone want to drop out. The table tennis competition demanded involvement, it was about taking part, it was about respect, and for

Cassie and Alison it was about something else as well. Although they would never say it out loud, because the army said they were all soldiers, they were all the same; Cassie and Alison wanted to beat as many of the blokes as they could. It was how they cemented their position within the gun crew and their whole chosen way of life.

This was how Cassie got to be playing Dave in the final match, the one which would decide what had now been elevated to Table Tennis Championship of the Universe.

Cassie to serve first in a raucous atmosphere and three winning points in a row upped the stakes immediately coaxing a huge response from the spectators.

"Come on Dave, mate. It's gonna be a whitewash!"

Two points pulled back. Change of serve. Cassie is weighing up Dave's game: heavy top spin forehand, always looking for a chance to smash a forehand drive. Play to his backhand. The lead changed hands several times but was always restricted to two points. Neck and neck throughout. Dave is concentrating on his game, the calls from the watching soldiers quieten, they know there is a real competition taking place and the time for jokes is over. Thirteen - twelve to Dave and Cassie to serve. She wipes the back of her arm across her forehead; sweat stains spread in her tee-shirt but she has her plan now: Dave has power, he could trade shots with anyone, but he doesn't like to be moved around the table whereas Cassie is nimble and quick. Three successive service points to Cassie. 15 – 13. The tent is silenced now, only the irregular sound pattern of the table tennis ball against bat and the toc toc bounce on the rigged-up table. Points are won alternately until Dave gets a lucky net cord and Cassie is momentarily thrown by such bad luck. 19 – 19 and no-one wants to call out and break the intensity of the moment, the epic struggle. Twenty points each, another change of serve and everyone knows that two clear points are needed for victory. Cassie to serve, aware of the frown of fierce application on Dave's face. She's been playing almost exclusively to his backhand; he's almost expecting it there now. Quickly, Cassie weighs up a gamble in her own mind, can she take him by surprise by playing to his strength, take him unawares? Your strength can be your weakness? The stakes are high, what are the odds-on success? Cassie serves a top spin serve to her opponent's backhand and his return is placed centre table: this is the time; it's now or never, all or nothing. She whips her shot across the net to Dave's forehand where he is ready and waiting to play his favourite shot. He returns a forehand drive with vicious topspin. Cassie, realising instantly that her gamble has not paid off, tightens and hits her shot too hard. The ball clears the table and Dave jumps back to allow it to bounce on the floor. 21 – 20 and victory in sight.

Later, Cassie would deny fiercely to herself, almost to the point of tears, that she was a "bottler". But the wind had been sucked from her sails. Her moment has gone. Her next serve lacks conviction and Dave pounces with another heavy drive. Cassie gets her bat to the ball but without direction, it hits the top of the net and bounces back heartbreakingly towards her. Cue uproar from the members of the gun crew. Their applause and cheering is generous and aimed at both participants in the encounter. Dave thrusts both of his arms up in the air revealing two black sweat patches in his armpits; a gesture of triumph, but mostly it's the action of a relieved winner.

"Champion! One chilled coke for me, I believe."

But he wasn't really responding to the good-natured ribaldry of his mates, his eyes were on Cassie, his worthy opponent. He walked around the table and shook her hand.

"Well played, Cas, mate."

Cassie smiled sportingly; it was all she could do before she turned to see Alison who had watched every minute, rooting for her friend. Cassie caught her eye and saw the curious combination of disappointment at her loss and pride in her efforts. She would say, "Hard luck," but no words were necessary.

## Chapter Twenty-One

# You Ought to be in Pictures

"I can give you a lift down into town." Mrs Jackson smiled proudly with the offer. Cassie was about to demur, not wanting Mum involved in everything. But Simon answered first,

"Thank you very much. It'll save us a bus fare."

"No problem. I forgot to pick up some milk so I'll drop you at the multiplex and then nip round to Asda. What about getting home? Are you going to give me a ring?"

Once again, Simon was first to respond. "No, that would be too much to ask. We'll find our own way home. Thanks anyway."

Cassie glanced gratefully towards Simon. Why was it that he was so at ease with adults? No awkwardness, no blurting out stupid things, he always seemed so relaxed. Just like Ali, Cassie thought, it must run in the family.

Simon turned down the offer of the front seat, preferring to fold his legs up in the back of the small saloon and sit alongside Cassie. They'd fumbled over seatbelts together and now their shoulders jostled and nudged as the car met each bend in the road. Cassie was looking forward to the evening and had chosen her smart, casual outfit accordingly, but she may not have been as excited as her mum who had seemed unusually bouncy all afternoon. She'd pushed some extra pocket money into Cassie's hand and insisted, "Pay yourself in and treat him to an ice cream."

Cassie knew where she was coming from. Mum had always had this independent streak and a belief in women standing on their own two feet.

"Gone are the days when we were just decoration," she'd said.

If there was any awkwardness it was when Cassie's mum drove off and left them at the multiplex where a few people were milling about and the coloured lights shone forlornly against the still bright early evening light. They weren't even sure which film they wanted to see or what time they all started.

"Come on," said Simon, taking her hand. "Let's find a film to watch." And they almost walked straight into the four girls from school.

"Cassie! Hi!"

"Hi!" Cassie knew the girls but they weren't great friends and they may not even have spoken to each other at school. The four girls all stood and looked at Simon and Cassie brazenly. They chewed gum and began to preen and prose as though edging towards the foreground of a photograph.

"Going to the flicks?" One of the girls asked laughing and talking unnecessarily loudly.

Cassie thought about answering, "No, going to get my head shaved," but she didn't. She just smiled and shouted back a "yeah," and the pair of them continued to walk on with Simon still holding her hand. And all of the girls had seen, and it if hadn't been the summer holidays, the whole school would have known the following day. Still, there was always texting and the ubiquitous reach of social sites. Cassie smiled to herself.

"Well, the choice is yours." They had seven films to choose from and they had narrowed it down to an action thriller, romantic comedy, a gory horror or a kids' cartoon. Cassie discounted the cartoon and the horror as not being her cup of tea at all, either of them. She quite fancied going to see the rom com as she liked those and Simon *had* said it was her choice so they could go and see that and wallow in the sentimental tosh knowing that whatever problems were thrown up, there's be a happy ending. But Simon though? What kind of tea did *he* like in his cup?

"I'll tell you what, let's go and see the action film."

"Sure?" Simon asked. "What if it's violent?"

"If it's too bloody I'll close my eyes."

Simon laughed and led her towards the cash desk.

They decided against ice cream and bought instead a huge tub of popcorn which they balanced between them taking turns to pick at the sticky, sweet confection, talking and laughing easily until the adverts and the trailers for forthcoming attractions finished. Then they settled to watch the main programme: a film about a guy who'd been framed at work, a high government official accused of murder and fraud and in the attempt to clear his name he'd had to assume a new identity and then sort out his enemies one by one. Of course, it helps if you are superbly fit and a secret martial arts champion and you can win all of the fights which suddenly come your way. Cassie found herself becoming bored with the film and she started to try and catch a glimpse of Simon who was gazing intently at the screen, neglecting now the bottom third of the popcorn tub. She wondered again about the rom com, maybe there was something to be said for a harmless bit of fluff. Maybe they should have gone to see that.

The evening was warm and mellow and still not dark when they stepped outside of the multiplex.

"Well, what did you think of that?"

It's the inevitable first question after watching a film. Cassie weighed up her answer carefully as she didn't think Simon was the type to take the polite response every time.

"It was okay, I suppose. But I expect it's the sort of film lads like more than girls."

"Why's that then?"

"Oh, because it showed a man overcoming all of the odds: a man with a good job, smart suits and everything, even a sexy secretary to help him out, but he's never happier than when he's fighting."

Simon laughed. "I can't say I blame him; he still gets the girl at the end. But may I remind you that it was your choice. I thought you might choose the sloppy romantic comedy."

And Cassie laughed too, and Simon didn't know why until she explained to him. It brought a confession from Simon,

"Look, I wasn't bothered about which film we saw tonight. I just wanted to spend some time with you."

It was like slipping down into a wonderful foamy bath, Cassie allowed the warm feeling to wash all over her as Simon continued, "Look, it's a nice night, should we forget about the bus and walk home?"

"But it's miles!" Cassie protested but only briefly. Walk all that way with Simon holding her hand? Yes, she thought she could agree to that.

It was confirmation, if that was needed, that Simon was really nice. It was as though they had known each other really closely for years and he wasn't just her best friend's brother. He didn't just talk about himself; he asked Cassie questions, he was interested in what she had to say. Had she thought about what she might do in the future?

"Footballer? Artist? Cook? You must have loads of choices."

Cassie shook her head. "I don't know. None of those are easy to get into, except maybe being a cook. I could flip burgers somewhere. But I'd really like to be one of those cooks on tv, the ones who do programmes from their own kitchen, "Cassie Jackson's Winter Warmer Recipes!"

Simon laughed, "You ought to do something where you can use that imagination of yours. You should go into acting."

"Do actors need imagination?"

"I think so. They have to imagine what it's like to be a different character, to be in a different world."

"Mm… I think I *could* do that," said Cassie ruefully.

"Well, I'd come and watch you on the big screen. I'd chew my popcorn and say to myself: *I know her*."

Cassie was quickly discovering that the thing about Simon was that he could easily join in with the nonsense conversations, sharing jokes and the daft ideas, but he also listened to serious comments, he didn't belittle them at all.

"What I'd really like to do," Cassie admitted, "I'd like to do a job where I thought I was helping other people."

Simon looked directly into her eyes, "Yes, that doesn't surprise me. I think you'd be good at that as well."

How quickly a long walk home could pass, and what a fantastic feeling it was to find someone who felt the same way as you did about all kinds of things, someone who seemed able to make sense of a crazy world, someone who didn't think a conversation was a competition but a joint venture where ideas could be explained and developed. Simon, Simon. Would Cassie ever admit how often when she'd been alone, she had whispered the name to herself? Simon.

As the summer night sky darkened, they approached their avenue. There were no kids out playing now, no cars on the quieter estate, just some noisy drinkers outside the Coach and Horses. Their own footsteps were barely audible on the pavement, just a gentle flip flapping. Simon steered Cassie towards a doorway set into a big garden wall and held her gently around the waist.

"I've enjoyed tonight. We'll do this again, right?"

Cassie could only nod, her vocal cords thickened, as Simon bent his head towards hers, she was unable to speak as his lips softly met hers and the kiss which she'd barely allowed herself to think about, the glorious kiss with Simon Jones, took place in the dusky warmth of that gorgeous July evening. Or at least that's how it should have been: a glorious memory to store up and replay night after night, every little detail: the wonderful warmth of a July evening, Simon's strength and gentleness, his desire and respect, but anxiety, swift and sudden, plucked up Cassie and dropped her into a panic.

"No. Stop!"

She pulled away from Simon; she wanted to get away, anywhere, somewhere safe. She didn't want to meet his eyes or see his face but she had caught that look of puzzlement on his face.

"You okay?"

She broke completely away from him in a half run, crossing the road without looking, making for her house. She had a start because Simon, so taken aback at this turn of events, had let her go, only deciding to overcome the indignity and chase after her as she threatened to disappear from view. He caught her on the corner only fifty metres from her house, bringing her to a stop with a restraining hand in the crook of her elbow.

"Cassie!"

She looked at him now and pulled her arm away.

"Let go of me."

Then she shouted the words which she felt sure would haunt her for ever,

"You were touching me.

## Chapter Twenty-Two

# RPGs and IEDs

The lines are blurred. Officially, it is stated that women in the British Army are not allowed to fight in the front line. But women soldiers are trained how to shoot a gun and trained to have no second thoughts should the need arise to use it. You or your enemy? You will not have time for scruples, for weighing up any delicate philosophical objections. And the next question would be where is the front line exactly? Not a problem when two armies face up to each other for attack and counter attack, but in Afghanistan it was a necessary state of mind to think that you were always in the front line whether you were lying in your bunk in the fort with the prospect of a rocket propelled grenade or mortar likely to scream down on you at any moment, or patrolling in the green zone tensed for the sniper's bullet or the terrors of the improvised explosive device. Even in the villages where patrols were meant to be a reassurance for the locals, a rider on a single moped or the driver of a rusty old truck chugging down the dusty road could be a suicide bomber ready to deliver his deadly cargo.

Women soldiers were often included in patrol duties and nothing was thought of it. Alison and Cassie were needed particularly if local women were to be questioned or searched; propriety demanded it. And in acting as an equal in these duties Cassie was well aware of the power of such role modelling. Look, we can take an equal part in society; we don't have to be secondary. Implicit in that was the assumption that women needed to be educated, that they had the right to vote and being respected didn't necessarily mean having your identity hidden under layers of clothing. But these women also had to be treated as suspects; a potential threat. Stories were legion about how the opposition would use women to conceal bombs and no-one needed reminding about how fraught these patrols and searches and questioning were.

How many times had Cassie admired the way Ali went about this particular business? Firmness and courtesy were needed as they were soldiers in someone else's country, village, home. Alison always worked with quiet authority, telling the interpreter what to say, "Just do as you're told and there will be no trouble."

And the local women would shuffle into the places they were supposed to be in with the young girls cowering protectively around their mothers' chadri. The men too, respected the instructions and only their eyes betrayed a sullen glare. Unperturbed, Alison would remove her helmet and shake her short, blonde hair as if to say, look at me, I am a woman doing my job. How Cassie longed to be able to convey the same self-assurance, the same authority.

That particular day they had visited three houses in the village following a tip-off about a possible weapons store. It had been a fruitless search; the element of surprise had been scant and it had diminished to nothing by the third house. The day was growing hotter and hotter and frustrations were bound to rise but the feeling was that such patrols and searches served a purpose. The villagers would not demonstrate any kind of welcome but the patrols were a reminder that the Taliban were being opposed and a form of life involving trading and agriculture was being maintained; the delicate balance, all the members of the patrol knew that the people with whom they were dealing could soon cease being traders or farmers as soon as conditions changed, as soon as the wheat and the poppy crop was harvested attention would turn elsewhere. As soon as the Taliban had demonstrable control, a village's allegiances would sway and the soldier's fate, as much as anyone else's, lay in this balance.

Cassie looked again at the women and the girls who stood silently watching these foreigners in their homes. How different their lives were, how Cassie had once admired their appearance; their dress of light linens which were so loose fitting: the trousers and long shirt with a belt. On special occasions fancier dresses were worn: coloured silk fabrics with gold threading and beads. Whatever the occasion, the clothing was designed to be loose so that the body outline could not be discerned by the lustful eyes of men. Cassie thought of how often she dressed with exactly that thought in mind: how might a certain man think of her in an outfit and was it tight enough? Now, of course, she dressed exactly like a man and, from a distance, no-one would ever look at her and think man or woman, they would look at her and think soldier. Meanwhile, the women of this village and many like it increasingly wore the chadri which covered the entire face except for a small region about the eyes. It was an ominous sign of growing Taliban influence.

The patrol emerged into the blistering heat, like walking into a slammed door, and re-formed in the street which led out of the village. Concentration had to be maintained and training procedures carefully followed. You are all relying on your mates to do their job properly. It was the mantra they had been repeatedly fed, the mantra they repeated to themselves. Doorways, windows and alleyways were all carefully watched as the patrol took it in turns to climb into the two Jackals, the heavily armed British Army patrol vehicle. Suspicious movement anywhere could mean a sniper about to claim a prize. A group of women or children was no guarantee that a shot wouldn't be fired using them as cover. Concentration was everything; well, concentration, training and luck.

Cassie was in the rear of the second Jackal. Seated alongside Dave, she had a restricted view out of the front windscreen and couldn't locate their precise position because she knew that routes were always being varied. Don't give your enemy a pattern which they can work to their advantage. What *was* familiar was the bumping and jolting on the un-metalled road. As part of the hearts and minds strategy a lot of building work had taken place: nurseries, schools, bridges and roads.

Look! We are here to help you people. They could do with a few more roads though Cassie thought as the desert-camouflaged vehicle lurched over another pot hole. The bumps and bruises, the tension, she'd wash it all out in the shower when they got back. She'd had a new bottle of shampoo and conditioner in the last post from home and she'd open that and spoil herself with the luxury, and maybe, if miracles do happen, the kitchen might be able to rustle up something other than mince for dinner. Cassie remembered fondly the turkey they'd had at Christmas and how the cooks had been brilliant in producing all the trimmings: roast and mashed potatoes, carrots, peas and gravy. And how, half a world away from friends, family and loved ones, they'd sung Silent Night and then feasted like kings. Now Cassie was allowing her mind to wander to thoughts of a succulent sirloin steak and a crispy green salad, oh and a glass of something red to wash it down.

Cassie was dimly aware of the dull thud and she half caught the sight of the bright flash of explosion and the leading Jackal leaping off the track in a slow- motion convulsion. Others reacted much more quickly. I.E.D: the danger which could strike anywhere without notice. The front vehicle was disabled; bodies had been flung clear and now lay motionless across the dusty earth. The training kicked in and other instincts were checked as the compulsion to run to your mates' aid had to be restrained. A radio report of the situation was crackled to base, the potential for contact with the enemy had to be assessed and then the distance between the two vehicles had to be mine swept for further I.E.D.s. Cassie knew all this and knew she had to operate in exactly the way she had been trained. She also knew that one of the soldiers lying prone, sprawled out in the choking dust, was Alison.

## Chapter Twenty-Three

# Flame Grilled Bangers

Cassie made the best spicy barbecue marinade anywhere in the world and the chops and chicken pieces had been carefully placed in amongst it and left overnight. With the whole pile of pork sausages which had been taken out of the fridge in readiness, there should be enough to feed everyone. Now it was time to make sure that all of the salads and hunks of bread were prepared and the barbecue was lit. It was absolutely vital to make sure that the flames died down to embers and then the meat could gently sizzle on the glowing charcoal bricks. Cassie looked around the garden furniture which had been set up on the patio and the neatly laid cutlery, plates and napkins which had been placed ready for action. Everything was in hand; all that was needed now was the arrival of the guests.

No sooner had the thought passed than the sound of voices and a garden gate closing announced the arrival of Alison and Simon closely followed by their mum and dad. Ali looked a lot stronger, getting back to her natural healthy appearance. Simon strolled easily behind her, tall, casual and very dishy. Mum and dad too, looked relaxed as well they might at the beginning of their long summer holidays. Alison's mum held up a bottle of wine.

"We've brought a friend, a nice crisp chardonnay. Shall I put it in the fridge?"

"Sure, go on in, you know where it is. Mum's in there somewhere."

"In the fridge?"

"No," laughed Cassie, "Although she could do with chilling out sometimes."

"I heard that, young lady." A mock reproach; Cassie's mum appeared at the doorway. "Hello everyone. Make yourselves at home. Drinks in the conservatory, nibbles in the bowls. Help yourselves. Cassie's got everything else under control. Come on Fran, let's find a bottle opener for your friend."

The two women stepped into the house, slipping easily into the pattern of a long-term friendship.

"You on nights, Bev?"

"That's right. Ten till six. In bed by seven, sleep till two, up and showered and here I am fresh as a daisy."

"I don't know how you keep it up." Fran Jones looked with genuine concern at her friend.

"I manage. I have to, don't I? It's Cassie I worry about. She's left alone more often than she should be."

"Cassie can cope. Look at the way she's dealing with that barbecue." The reassurance was welcome.

"I do hope so. She looks so drawn sometimes. Not with it. And she gets very uptight. She's got too much time for thinking. She's been so up and down lately; I worry about her."

She was rooting around in a packed cutlery drawer searching for the corkscrew and finding only the prong of a fork which jabbed into her finger. In a fit of annoyance, she picked out the fork and slammed it onto the kitchen worktop.

"Ouch!" She thrust her finger into her mouth and began to suck. "That hurt."

Fran Jones moved up closer to her friend and held her.

"It didn't hurt you that much though, did it?" What *is* the matter, Bev?"

It was the intuition that friends have about friends and now the gates were well and truly open, they could talk and share and support.

"No, it's Cassie, isn't it? I'm really worried about her. It's like she's not my girl anymore, she's miles away from me. At times, she completely withdraws. She's changed."

"Of course, she's changed, she's fourteen. It's what fourteen-year-old girls do."

"I know," Bev nodded, "but she's so far away from things. Sometimes it's like she's in a totally different world. The next minute, she's bright and chirpy with another plan on the go. She's like her dad in that respect: making plans, huge, impossible plans and then it's like she's hit a brick wall and it all comes to nothing."

All Fran could do was to continue to nod and prompt questions,

"Do you think she misses her dad?"

"Yes, of course, then sometimes I think she hates him for not being here. They are…they were, very close. It could be that, or it could be school. I thought there might be something bugging her at school and that maybe, when the holidays came, she'd lighten up a bit."

How do you discuss someone else's child? How do you talk to your friend about her daughter? Fran Jones was caught in the dilemma of wanting to offer constructive advice but she was also constrained by the bounds of friendship. Cassie Jackson was a great friend to her own daughter even though, like any friendship, it passed over rocky ground occasionally, but Cassie was a dreamer, often far removed in some fantasy or other, there was no point in telling her mother that, it was already widely known, but if the fantasies and mood swings were becoming darker, then yes, this was a problem and not one where she felt able to offer any worthwhile advice. She didn't really want to intrude. All was not well in this house. The fridge was stocked with more wine than was necessary for a barbecue and the glass recycling bin made it look like several parties had already taken place.

"Cassie and your Simon went out together the other night. How did that go? Did you hear anything about that?"

Now Fran had been offered something of an escape. She could shift the focus of the conversation and speak more freely without causing any offence.

"Did I hear anything? How likely is that? We're talking about Simon here. He's the original silent type, cards very close to his chest. Not a peep."

Bev smiled gratefully. She would have liked Cassie to come home and share every last detail. They could have had a girls' gossip, but it was not to be. If Fran hadn't heard anything about it, then it must have been okay and her doubts had been unnecessary. She finally located the corkscrew,

"Come on; let's show this little friend some action.

On the patio, Cassie was pre-occupied with cooking rather than anything else. The guests had taken seats at the table while the head chef expertly flipped the meat on the barbecue and called out her side of the conversation.

"I hope you guys are hungry, we've got enough meat here to feed a football crowd."

"Smells delicious. Anything we can do to help?" Mr Jones made the offer but sat back promptly; in his open-necked cotton shirt he was relaxed and cool. It was clear to see from where Simon got his amiable style.

Simon? Simon? He'd hardly spoken to her, and why should he? Not just now, this afternoon, but over the three days since they had been out together. Cassie could remember every single detail of the evening: sharing the popcorn, laughing at the adverts, slowly losing interest in the film and then the best of all, the long walk home. The best and the worst. How often she'd re-lived that kiss on the way home and how often she shuddered at the memory of what she'd done; pulling away like a stupid little girl. What was she frightened of? Simon was heavenly. She knew she ought to stay cool and not shout about Simon, because they weren't boyfriend and girlfriend or anything, they'd just been out one night and they were friends; friends who kissed. How difficult it was not to laugh and shout; how difficult was it to stay cool? Cassie wanted to see him every moment of every day but now it was difficult. Simon didn't do much texting and Cassie even felt diffident about going rounds to see Ali in case it looked too obviously like any old excuse. And what did Simon think now? What was he telling his mates? She knew boys liked to boast, she also knew they liked it when they had a weird story to tell.

Simon was sitting in their back garden right now not ten metres away from her. He'd said, "Hi!" He'd smiled and complimented her on her cooking skills: "Put me down for a banger," he'd grinned.

"Okay, you're a banger."

But Cassie was tortured by how much more they needed to say to each other. She remembered what he'd said three nights ago word for word: "I've enjoyed tonight. We'll do this again, right?" And the kiss of course, and how it felt so good to be held by him and then so wrong. Cassie had pulled away, a sudden wave of nausea sweeping over her.

"No. Stop!"

And the look of puzzlement on his face.

"You okay?"

How could she ever get that closeness back with Simon, how could she ever talk properly again with him when she would never be able to explain?

The two mums emerged from the conservatory. Cassie's mum handed Mr Jones a glass of wine.

"I took the liberty of choosing white for you."

"And why not? The sun's past the yard arm."

Everyone was smiling, everyone was happy, or almost everyone. Cassie was carefully piling the cooked meat onto a serving plate no longer as carefree as earlier. It was Simon, wasn't it? Simon who had made her feel top of the world, who had said they should go out again and then she'd virtually run away from him. Now he lolled carelessly in a sun chair, not having mentioned another date? Was he ignoring her? And if he was, who could blame him? Fat was beginning to drop on to the charcoal and spit back fiercely; smoke was rising into Cassie's eyes and try as she might she couldn't avoid rubbing them and then she knew they would have that terrible red, teary look.

"Well, thank-you for the invitation." Mr Jones held up his glass as if in a toast. "Are we celebrating anything in particular?"

"Oh, no. We just thought we would take advantage of the good weather and introduce a bit of the Continental into our life-style." And then Cassie's mum added, "Although Dan did say he might pop round this evening."

"Might?" Mrs Jones cast a quizzical look at Cassie's mum.

"Yes, might. We don't hold our breaths, do we Cassie?"

Cassie was making a difficult transfer of some chicken drumsticks away from the heat on the centre of the barbecue grill. The slogan on her apron said "Supercook" and she was affecting total concentration on the job in hand but those who looked at her closely saw the flicker of emotion in her face and saw that yes, she *did* hold her breath.

## Chapter Twenty-Four

# Soap Suds and Promises

Cassie was up to her arms in hot water and washing up suds, and deep in her own thoughts when she was startled by the tentative knock on the kitchen door. It was a little bit late for anyone to be calling at the back door, she thought reaching for a towel.

Simon looked sheepish proffering a DVD case to Cassie. "I meant to bring this round earlier to the barbecue, but I forgot. So, I popped back with it."

It was a long speech for Simon, he was almost gabbling.

"What is it?"

"*Ten Things I Hate About You.*"

"Charming!"

"Remember we spoke about it that night we went out."

The night they went out! Cassie almost jumped. "You'd better come in," she said leading him through the door into the kitchen. "Is that all you came back for, to give me the DVD?"

Simon took in the scene in the kitchen: the barbecue grid and utensils ready to be washed, the upturned glasses which stood sparkling on the draining board as the tiny bubbles slid off them. "I also came to see if you wanted a hand with the washing up." He added hurriedly.

"Liar!" Cassie was smiling but she could have bitten off her tongue feeling that the relationship between them was a little bit delicate to be calling him liar. "You all offered to help with the washing up before you left."

"It would have been rude not to."

"And it would have been rude of me to accept."

"But you'll accept now." Simon was gently insistent as he picked up the wire wool pad. "It needs a man to get off some of this dirt and grease."

"I beg your pardon!"

"I thought that might get a response. Come on, between us we'll have these done in no time."

He was as true as his word and before long a pile of glasses, cutlery and plates stood gleaming on the kitchen work top. All of the barbecue paraphernalia was also clean and ready for the next al fresco extravaganza.

"All done and dusted." Cassie smiled. "Thank you very much. Now, have you got time to watch that DVD?"

"I suppose so. Where's your mum?" Simon looked around as though expecting Mrs Jackson to jump out of a cupboard.

"She's gone to work."

"Won't she mind?"

"She gives me very strict instructions not to talk to any strangers or let them in. Are you strange?"

"Very," said Simon, "they don't come any stranger."

"Well, I'll just have to take that risk. Go and set up the DVD while I change this top, it stinks of smoke."

Cassie dashed up to her bedroom. There was no time for the full works of course but she tore off her tee shirt and picked out one of her best blouses from the wardrobe. It wasn't usually something she wore around the house but it was the first one she came to she told herself.

She flitted into her mum's bedroom for a quick and subtle spray of her perfume and then she paused. Simon Jones, *the* Simon Jones was downstairs in the front room of an empty house and she was ready. Sure enough, he had the DVD all set up and Cassie marched in with a glass in each hand.

"Left over from the barbecue," She indicated the two glasses generously filled with white wine. "Don't adults set us such a bad example? Come on, let's sit on the carpet." She settled down with her back resting against the sofa and patted the space beside her. "Will you join me in a glass of wine?

"Do you think we'll both fit into just the one glass?" He was laughing, they were both laughing, things were gonna be fine.

"Don't spill mind, otherwise you'll get me shot." Cassie took a sip from her glass and tried not to grimace. She didn't like wine; she didn't really like drinking to be honest but this seemed like the right thing to do: a shot of Dutch courage perhaps. She shuffled along closer to Simon.

"So, what's this film about?"

"It's a modern take on The Taming of the Shrew. You said you were doing it at school."

"Shakespeare?" Cassie was doubtful.

"Yeah, you'll enjoy it."

But she didn't enjoy the film. She didn't get it, she wasn't concentrating. Neither, it seems, was Simon. Eventually, he took a long pull from his glass to finish off his wine almost like he was drinking beer and then he moved both his own and Cassie's glass onto the nearby coffee table. Cassie watched as he carefully made sure the glasses were on coasters. Then he turned to Cassie.

"That night we went to the pictures. On the way home, you sort of ran away from me."

It was the moment Cassie feared. "There was no sort of about it," she said. "I ran off. I don't know why. I was an idiot."

"You're not an idiot." Simon was quick to reply as he awkwardly adjusted his position to ease an arm around her shoulders. "It's just that if I kiss you now, will you run off again?"

"I've nowhere to run to, this time, have I?"

Simon leaned in towards Cassie and paused momentarily as their faces were a whisper away from each other then he put his lips to hers and began to kiss, slowly and tenderly as the DVD played, the American High school kids followed their scripted destinies and the noisy soundtrack hammered out. It was the moment Cassie had longed for and dreaded. It might be difficult but she wasn't going to mess up this time. She only had to concentrate; it was Simon beside her, dishy Simon. This was okay, this was natural and nice, especially when he let his tongue gently explore like that and his hands stroked her like he was handling something precious. Then, oh my God, he began carefully unfastening each of the buttons, working his way tenderly down the front of her blouse. She'd only partially tucked it in anyway but now he pulled it clear from the waist of her trousers. She felt strangely exposed but unable or unwilling to do anything about it. She wanted to run her hands under *his* shirt but she couldn't but she couldn't adjust her position without falling over. He was letting his fingers play over her white belly and her sides, murmuring all of the time, saying that she was lovely as his hands worked their way upwards for the gentlest of caresses. Dimly, she was aware of the change which had come over him. Were all boys like this? He was no longer laughing and joking, he was solemn and earnest, muttering things which she could no longer make out and emitting soft groans. Then his hands swept smoothly around her back and he began to tug and fumble with her bra strap. Now she did have to move or else she would fall over into an undignified heap.

"Simon, hang on." She was trying to help but she'd halted the momentum and spoiled the moment. She reached out to try and reassure him but he misread her actions.

"Sorry. Too far?" Although he tried to pull away, she held him.

"No, no. Gosh, are you cold? You're shivering!" She could hardly keep the surprise out of her voice. It was the height of summer, after all.

"No, I need to use the bathroom though." Simon scrambled to his feet calling, "Don't go away, will you?" as he left the room and then she heard his tread on the stairs. Wondering where on earth he thought she might go to, Cassie sat in the front room by herself. She reached for the remote and switched off the film; she tidied herself up, refastened her blouse and tucked it back into her trousers. Not to do that, she thought, would be too loose. Then she flopped into an armchair and waited.

Although he hadn't used the toilet, Simon flushed it then went over to the sink, ran the cold tap and splashed water over his face. He leaned over to the bathroom mirror and took a long look at the strange figure who stared back. It was the strange figure, someone he barely recognised, who had just been doing the sort of things he'd thought about doing for ages. It had been a little bit awkward and a little bit uncomfortable but it had been just as he imagined it to be although he'd been much clumsier than he'd pictured. But it was a golden opportunity and who was to say that the moment had passed? There was a girl sitting downstairs alone in the house and she'd seemed keen; nervous perhaps, but keen. She was a girl he'd heard his mates talking about in approving fashion. This wouldn't do his reputation any harm. Why not go back down and pick up where they had just left off? He only had to rid himself of the absurd notion that he wished his friends were there now to see him. He dried his face on a towel and took one more hard look at himself in the mirror and then made his way back down the stairs.

When he returned to the room, Cassie smiled at him a little bit shyly, a little bit knowingly.

"This is a bit weird," he said to her, "with your mum not being here and everything."

"Would you rather she was sitting on the sofa?"

"No," he had to laugh, "You know what I mean. It shouldn't feel as though we are doing something wrong, something secretive."

"Yeah, I think I know what you mean." Cassie walked towards him and put her arms around his neck. "But we weren't doing anything wrong. Not me and you."

"No, but I'm gonna go home now, anyway. But let's do stuff."

"I thought we *were* doing stuff!"

"Yeah, and it was nice, but I mean let's go the pictures again or something."

"Is that you asking me out, smooth talker?"

"Yeah."

Cassie squeezed him and led him towards the door. "You know what this means, don't you?"

"What do you mean?"

"You're running off from me. You've just scored your equaliser."

He stopped and kissed her again, much more chastely than before. "I won't run off again.

"Neither will I." She kissed him back.

## Chapter Twenty-Five

# Broken Bodies and Choppers

"Ali! Ali! Stay with us Ali!"

The trained medic in every patrol lugs around the first aid kit as well as the normal kit carried by soldiers. Most often they are called upon to treat heat exhaustion, supply glucose for low blood sugar, but their key training is in gunshot and blast injuries and they know that the first few minutes of treating such injuries are vital.

"Ali, don't fall asleep!"

Voices rise with the tension. The victim has to remain conscious; the first aid has to be applied quickly, and meanwhile the patrol knows that the longer they stay in that place, the greater the chances of contact with the enemy on their terms. Some disused buildings to their left flank could be suitable cover from which to mount a small arms attack. The Green Zone, not too much further away with its tall growing crops and irrigation channels is an ideal position for opposition forces to launch mortars or rocket propelled grenades and then melt away before reprisals.

"Cassie! Come and talk to her. Keep her talking."

Cassie knelt down by Ali's head. What to say? She had no idea, but anything was better than nothing. Keep her talking, keep her conscious.

"You're doing fine, Ali."

"It's my leg, isn't it?"

"Yeah, you'll be fine. Stay with us. Dave's sorting you out."

Would she be fine? The patrol had responded as trained. Everyone knew the procedure: treat the casualty, prevent additional casualties and complete the mission. And Dave *was* treating the casualty; Dave the table tennis champion of the Universe was now expertly following the procedural steps, making the assessment of airway, breathing and circulation and a tourniquet had been applied to stop the bleeding; the blood which pulsed, vivid and bright scarlet with every beat of Ali's heart. Blood, so much blood.

"Is it bad?"

It was a good sign that Alison was talking, now she needed reassurance as the ugly wave of battlefield trauma and shock was due to sweep over her.

"You'll be fine. We've radioed for a chopper and soon you'll be travelling in style."

Cassie knew that the help she had to offer had to remain professional help: calm and detached. They had been friends for years; close, best of friends, but emotion had to be excluded now. She was doing her job and wouldn't allow herself to worry or speculate about the amount of blood. Of course, Ali would be fine; didn't she always emerge with a graceful smile of triumph?

Dave continued to work, he still had options about the bleeding, direct pressure was one, or applying a hemostatic dressing. His other concern was to create intravenous access for a catheter. The casualty would need morphine and then the helicopter boys could take it from there.

"How's she doing, Cassie?"

"She's fine, aren't you Ali? Tell him, tell him you're ready to whip him at table tennis."

Alison, her face smeared in dust, and tired now could only grimace. Cassie, desperately trying to think of more aimless banter allowed traitorous thoughts to creep into her head: she was supposed to be supporting Ali but it was her own selfish thoughts that began to preoccupy her: how far away from everything she felt now; despite email connections and calls on mobile phones, these endless horizons, the sand, dust and shouting of soldiers only reminded her that she was in a foreign country thousands of miles from where she called home and all the mates in the world couldn't prevent the sickness of loneliness settling on her.

"Ali! Keep talking, Ali. You didn't tell me about that photo in your last letter."

It couldn't happen, could it? This barren landscape of sand, stones and desert, of dust and flies, of sweat constantly trickling below body armour, of cold, cold nights, this was no place to die.

Privately, everyone had thought about being a casualty and the extent of possible injuries. They all knew stories about wounded soldiers and how well they recovered, about the amazing advances in prosthetic limbs and the incredible levels of mobility achieved by amputees. High profile examples of these completed long-distance charity walks and marathon runs and were hailed as courageous heroes. Less well publicised were the stories of wounded soldiers who didn't recover, whose injuries went beyond the physical, those who turned to alcohol or domestic violence for salvation or simply slipped into a dark whirlpool of mental instability. Hell, you didn't need to be injured for that; these dangers lurked for all soldiers after tours of duty. It was the sacrifice which didn't earn any medals. Cassie had dwelled on these points and reached the conclusion that many others before her had reached: it might be better to be killed in action rather than wounded and disabled.

Tension and stress are inevitable; use these as triggers for increased performance. This is what they had done, how they had dealt with the prospect of being so exposed with one vehicle disabled and two casualties. The distant sound of the helicopter, the small black dot in the sky growing bigger, was a profound relief though not an excuse for relaxation, there was still a job to be done. The pilots would no more like to be sitting exposed in this area than the patrol. Landing and taking off were fraught operations; the loading would need to be efficient and quick.

Everything happened in a blur of rotating blades and swirling sand. The casualties were despatched and once more, after an eardrum bursting take off, the chopper rose into the sky, made a wide sweeping curve receding into the cobalt blue sky and soon resumed its appearance of a diminishing black dot. Time between incurring the casualties and the evacuation was an amazing eleven minutes. Later, as reports were being considered, a great deal of satisfaction would be taken from this. For now, though, above the fading chatter of the helicopter, Cassie heard the report being radioed to base: "Confirm, amputation to left leg below the knee."

Professional to the core and highly trained, Cassie thought about her friend and colleague with a shattered leg, stretchered on the floor of a helicopter flying through the sky of this foreign land, carried towards a list of official statistics of wounded or killed in action, and she fought every bodily instinct to lean over into the sand and spew.

## Chapter Twenty-Six

# England, My England

Cassie was perturbed by any fuss, hating shiny welcome home banners and bundles of balloons tied to the front door. Nor could she cope with a quiet life, the expectation that she could just settle in to what was regarded as normal. She was tetchy, ill at ease and unable to relate to friends at home whose lives revolved around jobs, shopping and bringing up babies when Cassie's life had centred on the likely possibility of taking careful aim through a gun sight, focussing on a human target and shooting them dead. If anything, returning home and settling back into life in England after a tour of duty was as difficult as anything experienced by veterans whilst posted in Afghanistan.

Cassie missed the others, missed the banter and the piss-taking. Around her mates there was no need to try and explain; there was no need to bite your tongue when someone in a pub was expressing an opinion about Afghanistan. How could the saloon bar thinkers possibly know what it was like? How did a nine to five job entitle someone to an opinion about a country three and a half thousand miles away with a lifestyle and customs dating back at least a century? And worst of all, Cassie couldn't bear being feted: she wasn't a hero, nor was she brave, she just knew she would do anything for her mates, and knew all too clearly the lengths to which they would go for her. The war might not make sense, civilian attitudes in England might not make sense; the only thing that did add up was the re-affirming power of friendship; of being a mate.

Which was why, home on leave, Cassie chose mostly to be alone. People around her tried to understand, they made allowances, "You don't know what she's been through out there," but eventually their tolerance was tinged with hurt and resentment; very well, she could get on with her life and they would get on with theirs.

And now, Cassie stood at the war memorial in the small Wiltshire town. It was a morning with a distinct chill in the air, the mist lifting gently from the surrounding roof tops suggesting that summer's days were numbered. The main road by which she stood was the road to R.A.F. Lyneham where military aircraft made their landings and slow-moving convoys were then despatched through England's rolling countryside, squeezing between the villages of Tockenham and Tockenham Wick into an otherwise unremarkable market town and onto the motorway towards the golden-stoned city of Oxford, the seat of learning, the ancient focus of aspiration, the site of the armed forces department of pathology. Cassie had chosen not to wear her uniform. In this crowd of a thousand people gathering in silent respect, Cassie wanted to be alone; let people look at her black trousers and sweat top and then pass on. There was nothing to be read into her appearance; no sign, no symbols, just let her be.

Not so the people around her. There were families done up in their best clothes: young boys in ill-fitting jackets and ties, girls constrained in dresses they would normally wear for weddings, and old men, lots of old men. Next to Cassie a man had hobbled painfully to the pavement's edge for a good view. He wore a crisp white shirt and a regimental tie, black blazer with a row of medals above the breast pocket. He didn't wear a coat although as the summer was fading, surely a coat was needed to ward off the chill. He was short of breath, gasping in the cold air but he had left his mobility scooter parked by a shop window as a matter of principle; for what was about to happen, he wanted to stand. He wasn't alone as amongst the crowd of families and townspeople who were putting their normal lives on hold for a while were groups of ex-servicemen, some of whom wore medals and carried flags, others who had simply turned out as a matter of respect.

A hush fell over the crowd almost as though a message had been sent in advance running up the main street towards the war memorial. The tolling of the church bell was confirmation that the convoy of hearses and police motorbikes had stopped outside the church. It was the signal for the ex-servicemen to defy the years and stand ramrod straight as a silent respect fell like a lowered flag over the town, the only noise was the mournful monotone of the church bell and the powerful police motorbikes straining at the leash of low revs.

Cassie wanted to be there at this town that stands duty for all England, not to speak or announce her own experience but just to be there as the cortege made its slow progress to the war memorial. The old soldiers maintained their parade ground stance but the sight of the stately black cars and the first glimpse of the coffins was too much for the families who had to grip each other, supporting themselves against the sudden intensified assault of grief. Wailing and moaning rose from the mothers, fathers, the widowed and those who had seen the coffin of their boyfriend or girlfriend carried before them.

Cassie stayed until the sombre convoy moved on, until the church bell stopped tolling and the crowd slowly dispersed. This small town had done its bit, ensured that a respectful observance had taken place and maintained the pledge that the dead soldiers would be remembered. Now she looked around for the pub, noting again how often she said or thought the phrase, "I need a drink." In much the same way that some of her army mates on leave doubled or tripled their cigarette consumption, ran up debts with the bookies or toured the pubs at night where they knew they could pick up a fight.

She stepped into the Golden Lion and realised that many of the drinkers had attended the same ceremony and there was no question of life returning immediately to normal. The pub landlady was respectfully dressed in black and the normal lounge bar chatter was suppressed. Cassie bought herself a whisky telling herself that it was only to warm her up. She looked around for a space, ideally a table in a quiet corner, thinking she was the first there but she was wrong. How had she missed the increasingly frantic waving from the table over by the big fireplace? She pushed her way through the customers spotting that there was one spare chair by the table. She put down her drink and slumped gratefully in to the winged armchair.

"How did you not see me? I was waving like an idiot."

"Sorry," said Cassie automatically averting her eyes from the sticks placed by the chair and the left leg of the track suit bottoms which she knew covered an artificial lower leg. "How are you, Ali?"

"Champion, absolutely champion. And yourself?"

## Chapter Twenty-Seven

# Home is where I want to be

Perhaps it was the sudden arrival of summer weather, July bursting in with some brilliant sunshine and then settling for hot and sultry. It was the type of weather which puts a slow brake on everything, which inhibits action and brings life to a slow crawl. Or maybe it was the arrival of the heavy clouds and oppressive atmosphere which only a major thunderstorm could clear. Either way, Cassie was listless and out of sorts. She was fidgety and looking for some form of release. She'd already been for a bath, loading it with her favourite foams and pampering herself with powder afterwards. But maybe she'd run the water too hot as the bath hadn't had the desired effect and she still felt at a physical and mental loss. She had her lightest cotton dressing gown draped around her but she couldn't settle to the soap opera which deeply absorbed her mum. One of the characters had been "inside". Now he found out that his wife had been unfaithful.

Cassie stood up from the armchair. "I'm going to have an early night."

A quick glance through the window showed that there was no need to draw the curtains yet as it was still a broad summer's evening. It certainly was going to be an early night and Cassie's mum was startled.

"Are you alright, love?"

"Yeah, I'm just a bit tired, I think."

"Shall I get you something? Do you need a paracetamol?"

"Mum, don't fuss. I'm just a bit tired that's all."

"You said you'd wait for me." The soap opera character continued his bleating, "But you're just a slag."

Cassie's mum picked up the remote and turned down the volume on the tv. "I'm not fussing. Just concerned, that's all."

"Well, I'm okay. Just tired. I don't need anything."

"Okay,, if you say so, love. I'll pop in and see you later."

Cassie disappeared beyond the sitting room door leaving her mum to think how much she'd like to go and tuck her daughter into bed next to her favourite teddy. But those days were gone, long, long gone. Now she watched her leaving the room and once again began fretting about her.

Even with the curtains drawn it was too light for sleep. Cassie had picked up her book and then tossed it aside before she'd read a page. She turned to a gossipy magazine but that soon went the same way. So, she lay in her bed and looked at all of her football posters on the wall and all of her drawings; the cat pictures had still not been taken down and she sighed to herself, what was it all about? Why could she not shake off this dreadful cloud which hovered over her every move? Why could she not tell anyone about the dark episodes which stalked her every living moment? She lay down and closed her eyes to chase the elusive sleep. And then she opened them again. What time was it now? Had she slept at all? She wasn't at all surprised by the movement in her bedroom.

"Trouble sleeping, Miss?"

He hadn't changed at all. He was still packed into the uniform which was too big for him. He still looked as though all of his personality was subsumed by his military regalia. Private William Bell stood proudly and smartly to attention.

"It's you again. What do you want, Will?"

"If you don't mind me saying so Miss, you are sometimes a little abrupt in your tone of voice."

Cassie was astonished. "I'm sorry. Would you like me to be a little more demure?"

"I only mention it because young men who might like to come calling might find it something of a deterrent."

"Oh Will, you're such a love, but you are a little bit out of touch. Young men don't come a calling."

Clearly, expressing his own views in such a forthright manner was something with which Private William Bell was not comfortable. "Begging your pardon again Miss, I'm surprised that you don't have any gentlemen callers."

"No, Will, things are a little different now, that's all."

It was as though he hadn't heard because he ploughed on anyway. "But if that is the case, I would be very proud if you allowed me the honour of calling on you."

"No, Will, that's lovely, and I would be equally proud to be seen walking with you. You might be the most handsome young man I know. You're certainly the smartest, but things are a little bit complicated at the moment."

"Is there are gentleman to whom you are attached?"

"Look Will, there is someone I really fancy..." Cassie searched for a better way of expressing herself when she saw the look of bafflement on Will's face. "...I mean there is someone I am rather fond of, I'm sweet on him."

"In which case, I offer my apologies for my untimely comments. I assume this gentleman's intentions are honourable."

"Oh Will, really, do try and relax a little bit. I'm sure one day you will be a fine young man for somebody but do try and remember that the young ladies you refer to are capable of thinking and speaking for themselves, and they want a little bit of fun before bothering with honourable intentions. To your ears that may sound a bit abrupt but it is the way the world is now. What are you doing here anyway? Is that why you came to see me?"

"I can't answer that Miss."

"Look there you go again, all trussed up like a turkey ready for the oven. Can't or won't? Why don't you let yourself go a little bit instead of bringing me the same old stuff: *I was defending the Empire, serving the Queen*"? Cassie had been flattered by Will's attention and suggestion but now her voice betrayed her tiredness, her too-hot-to-sleep tetchiness.

"It was a fine thing I did." Will stood even straighter.

"No, it wasn't. It was a stupid thing. You had friends and family." Exasperated, Cassie raised her voice even further. "You had a life on the farm, a life with the animals which you loved and you gave it all away to go *fighting*." She spat out this last word with venom.

"With respect Miss, I don't think that's a subject which may be beyond the experience of a young woman."

With surprising energy, Cassie lifted herself out of the bed and she picked up the first thing that came to hand, an antique silver snuff box. "Are you telling me that girls…women, aren't allowed to speak? Should we remain dumb? Are we china dolls to be wrapped in cotton wool? And she hurled the box at the impassive figure of the soldier standing in her room. "Now go away and leave me alone!" Cassie's voice had reached screaming pitch. The snuff box soared through the thin air of the empty bedroom, where there was no longer a soldier in full uniform standing to attention, and scored a tear through the smiling face of a footballer, gouged an ugly scar into the wallpaper and then fell with a thump onto the carpet. "That's right, go on, get lost!" Her intense frustration remained. How could she get this stuffy boy to have a close look at himself? How could she get him to see through the propaganda he'd been fed and which he'd obediently swallowed? How could she get into that thick head of his? He wasn't always right; the world was much more complicated than he made it sound. Doing one's duty, doing the right thing was not the answer to everything. The slow build-up of atmospheric pressure which had been taking place all day now erupted from within Cassie as she raged at the uniformed soldier with his preoccupation with duty and his suffocating obsession with manners. "Get out!"

The storm raged upstairs while downstairs on tv the row between soap opera characters continued.

"You've no idea what it's bin like. I've scrimped and saved, I haven't bin out at all, just so's I could go and see you every fortnight in that stinkin' dump. Treated like dirt on the way in and on the way out. And all I got was to see you sittin' feelin' sorry for yourself." Loud screaming now, the prelude to a dramatic slap. "You've no idea what it's bin like for me."

Shouting from the screen, acceleration towards the explosive cliff-hanger pronouncement, the credit roll and the theme tune, but Cassie's mum couldn't possibly watch any longer as she became aware of the shouting in her own house as well as the banging and clattering, from Cassie's bedroom. Without pausing to switch off the television she jumped from her chair, ran from the lounge and began to leap up the stairs two at a time to see what on earth was going on.

She flung open the bedroom door and was dumbfounded by the sight before her. Cassie was in her light cotton summer pyjamas, the ones with the teddy bear print which were too young for her really but to which she still clung. This though was no little girl stamping around the bedroom but a possessed spirit in demented action. She was tearing at all the posters she'd once so carefully pinned up, yelling and screaming at the smiling footballers, the contented looking cats and the pop stars she'd emulated.

"I hate you. All of you. Hate! Hate! Hate!"

The bedroom was being trashed; posters and wallpaper had been torn from the wall, books, ornaments and keepsakes had been thrown to the floor and a camcorder and tripod had been sucked up and then discarded into a chaotic mess by the whirlwind.

"Cassie! Cassie! What is it?"

The girl barely recognised her mother but continued in her rage picking up some small framed photographs from her bedside table to hurl at the pock-marked wall.

"Cassie!" This time her mother had to do more than simply repeat a name continually. She strode across the room ignoring the debris which littered the carpet and grabbed her daughter in a smothering embrace which thwarted any further physical violence being inflicted on the room.

And they stayed in that position for some time until the rage abated leaving only the torrent of tears; the calm after the storm.

"Cassie. What is the matter? What's caused all of this?"

Maybe she ought to have shouted, maybe she ought to have been angry at the wanton vandalism, the sheer unthinkingness of it all, but she wasn't. Cassie's mother already had an inkling that whatever the problem was, it was somehow part of payback time. Her daughter who had had to bear all of the responsibility for looking after herself so often while she had worked her shifts, who'd been expected to behave like an adult when she was only fourteen for goodness sake, had finally begun to crack, and the guilt which had stalked her mother for so long had now begun to make its presence more urgently felt. Without releasing her grasp, she edged Cassie towards the bed and gently they both lowered themselves to sit on the edge where Cassie turned her face towards her mother's chest and continued to weep. It needed time. Time for the tears to subside before any talking could be done, time for body and soul to be collected before any rapprochement could be made, and only slowly did Cassie begin to slur out any words of explanation.

"It's him, isn't it?" Private William Bell. He just can't see it, can he?"

Her mum had decided just to let her talk, to let her get this out of her system, whatever *this* was, but she couldn't resist asking the obvious question,

"Who's William Bell?"

"A soldier, he left his friends and family to go and fight in the Crimea."

"The Crimea?"

"Yeah, and he thinks he did a good thing, he thinks he served his Queen and country."

"But..." Now Cassie's mum couldn't find any words she wanted to use.

"But he didn't. Fighting and war don't ever solve anything, do they?"

"Well, no, I don't suppose they do."

Snuffling into her mother's top, Cassie's words were barely decipherable, and even if they were, her mum struggled with the apparent lack of logic.

"Look at Ali for instance, going out to help those people and then getting her foot blown off by a cowardly attack."

"Cassie," her mother recovered herself. "What on earth are you talking about? Alison had a nasty bout of summer flu, that's all. She's okay now. You're not making any sense!"

"No, none of it makes sense, does it? Sending young kids thousands of miles to a foreign country, telling them they're fighting for a good and honourable cause, doesn't make any sense." Everything was gushing out now in an unstoppable torrent where fact, fiction, reality and daydreams merged in one giant tidal wave. "And those boys in the park? Why did Simon say it was his ball? It was my ball and he told those boys it was his. He didn't have to say that."

"He maybe thought he was doing the right thing, love."

"Well, I didn't do the right thing. I swore at them. I used the "f" word. I never use the "f" word."

Cassie's mum increased the strength of her hug. "No, you don't, but it was a difficult situation for all of you."

"I swore at him because he groped my breasts."

Cassie's mum hadn't pried into the story about the confrontation in the park, reasoning that it was all part of growing up. You can't be everywhere to protect your kids. She'd thought it best to let them deal with it themselves; she'd deliberately not interfered. Now, what she had just heard about this story made her realise that sometimes when it came to interfering you were damned if you did and damned if you didn't.

"Cassie, if that boy did that, you should have reported it to the police. That's a sexual assault."

At first, she tried to pretend that she didn't hear Cassie's response, after all her voice had been so quiet and snuffling. It was even quieter now but she couldn't pretend any longer, not now when Cassie's words were audible and they sliced through any pretence like a bayonet.

"Well, he's not the only one, is he?"

Slowly, Cassie's mum pulled herself away from Cassie in order to allow her daughter to lift up her head and they could look each other face to face when she asked the next all-important question.

"Cassie, has someone else been… touching you?"

And her eyes were wide with anxiety and fear when Cassie nodded her response.

She had to ask who? And where? And when? It needed to be done delicately, she had to fight the surge of nausea she felt in her own throat in order to offer some belated protection to her daughter, but they were interrupted by a figure standing in the bedroom doorway with a sheepish grin on his face. He carried three pizza boxes in his outstretched arms.

"I'm sorry, I did knock but I got no answer. I knew you were in so I let myself in with my key. I didn't know if you'd eaten, I've brought some supper." His voice trailed off as he realised that this wasn't a moment for talking about late suppers. "What's been going on her? It looks like a battlefield."

The pizzas would grow cold. He didn't know the half of it. When he didn't turn up, he was unreliable, when he did turn up as part of a surprise, it all went badly wrong. He always thought that it wasn't easy being a dad at the best of times; it was so easy to slip from the straight and narrow and find yourself doing things which you ought not to do no matter how good your intentions might be. Now he was being brought face to face with a problem which had been submerged but which now raised its enormous, ugly head out of the black water and there was no hiding place and no denial, he knew now with certainty that he had to face his full responsibilities.

## Chapter Twenty-Eight

# He Told Me to Take Off My Top and I Did

They were always being told: school, lessons and homework are all-important, there is no time to lose and you need to work to the best of your ability all of the time. Targets, results, surpassing targets and adding value largely ruled their lives. There was no let up at all unless you were called out of class for an errand or to become one of Mr Brown's girls. That is to do a small job around school for Mr Brown when you could find yourself showing visitors around the school, carrying deliveries, helping to set out for a Parents' Evening or even doing some tidying up. These occasions were secretly relished by the pupils: officially sanctioned time outs when the said jobs could be stretched out and more of the lesson than was strictly necessary could be missed were always a bonus.

Recently, Cassie had found herself regularly chosen to be one of Mr Brown's girls whereas Alison was never chosen; another reason for Cassie's pleasure. And it seemed as though Mr Brown was conniving in the missing of lessons.

"Now, we don't want to miss more of Humanities than is strictly necessary," he'd say with a knowing wink and Cassie realised that there was another side, a human side to her headteacher as not many of the subject teachers would let the mask drop and reveal a little of their feelings. Mr Brown would.

"I've got a headache that's been pounding away all day," he'd said as he closed the blinds to his office throwing the room into an intimate shade. Having shown some prospective parents around school, Cassie sat in an easy chair waiting for any additional jobs that may need doing.

"Reach up. Help yourself to a glass of water."

Cassie looked at the jug of water and the glass beakers placed on the small tray on the coffee table before her and decided not to accept. She looked around at the bookshelves neatly stacked with boring looking books and files. A few notices were pinned in orderly fashion to a board and three big framed pictures hung on the walls. One of them Cassie quite liked, it had what looked like rows of houses on a hillside which stood below a giant full moon. The sky was dark blue and the moon a blood-red orange. It was this picture which kept attracting her attention as there was little else of note in the office. Mr Brown must have had the tidiest desk in the school. Its bare wooden surface shone, and on it there was only an open writing pad and two pens in a stand as well as a couple of photo frames but from where she sat, Cassie couldn't make out the actual photos.

"I knew you would do a good job." Praise from Mr Brown and once again that feeling of being made to feel special, that there was a bond between a Year 9 pupil and the Head of the whole school. "I'll keep you on my list of pupils who will never let me down."

The office seemed to be safely cocooned from the rest of the school, no noises here and no raised teachers' voices, badly played musical instruments or banging from the Resistant Materials workshops. Unnecessary really, but Mr Brown lit a desk lamp and flooded the office with an amber glow.

"Well, no more jobs after all. We'd better let you get back to lessons."

Cassie stood, hiding her disappointment that her few minutes of being special were coming to an end.

"But wait a minute; I didn't let you show parents around looking like that, did I?"

Cassie flushed and unsuccessfully tried to adjust her school tie, pushing it back up to her top button.

"You pupils; I don't know, always with ties slipping down and shirts untucked."

It was his jovial tone but Cassie was conscious now of how she was failing to pass muster.

"Here, let me have a go. I've put on one of these every day of my working life. I must be some sort of expert by now. Let's have you looking shipshape."

Cassie tried and failed to maintain control of her own smartening up process. He tugged her tie completely free of her collar.

"I'll tell you what, let's start from scratch. Take off your jumper."

Cassie wore a forced smile, trying to accept that this uniform ritual was a game between teachers and pupils and an acceptance would never be reached about what constituted *smart*, but she was also shamed by his close attention again. Clumsily she removed her jumper knowing that now she had also messed up her hair and she was thrown into further disarray.

As soon as she was outside in the corridor feeling shaken and weak, Cassie tortured herself with the knowledge that she had known that would happen and that she could have made sure that she was impeccably smart before she even went into his office. She could have made sure it didn't happen again, but she'd gone in like a fly being enticed into a web, and he'd fastened her tie right up to below her chin, elaborately smoothed down her shirt and tucked it into the waistband of her trousers. He pretended to care, he pretended to be on her side but he had great lumbering fingers that delved, foraged and touched. Again, again and again she stood alone in this undertow of misery.

She clung to the corridor wall by the giant school logo with the weight of the last few minutes pressing down and crushing her. What had happened was wrong. She knew that, so why hadn't she tried to prevent it? She needed to find the nearest toilet and quickly. She needed to find an empty cubicle where she could kneel on the cold floor and hang her head over a bowl.

"Thank you, Cassie. You've been very brave and you've done exactly the right thing."

Kerry was speaking to her gently but firmly. She'd introduced herself as a Family Liaison Officer. Another police officer sat slightly back from her who didn't say anything at all but he occasionally smiled in an encouraging way like a kindly uncle. Mum and Dad were with her but they too sat silently having been asked to let Cassie tell the whole story herself. So, she'd done her best, trying not to cry at the bits where she felt particularly ashamed. It wasn't until Kerry asked her about boyfriends that she lost control. She told her about Simon and how they'd been to the cinema once, and no, he hadn't tried to do anything.

"We kissed, that's all." Cassie was anguished by the thought of her parents sitting behind her. And no, she wasn't sexually active. Why was she asking these questions?

Mum leant forward and reached for Cassie's hand giving it a gentle squeeze.

It was late when they got back home from the police station. They had travelled through the hot summer's night in a silent car, each of them with their own thoughts and when they got back inside the house Mum had gone straight up to Cassie's room and cleared up the worst of the mess. But Dad had said, "Let's try not to worry about it too much now. Get yourself a good night's sleep and we'll talk about everything in the morning."

These were the last brief thoughts that Cassie had that night as the sleep which had eluded her earlier now closed in to take her in a gentle embrace. The great weight which she'd been carrying around with her had been shifted. Not entirely removed, but lifted sufficiently for Cassie to be able to take some deep breaths again, to feel free and alive. And Dad had said, "We'll talk about everything in the morning," hadn't he? It was the last thing which drifted into and out of Cassie's conscious mind: Dad was going to be around in the morning.

## Chapter Twenty-Nine

# Neverland

What a change in the world! It had rained overnight and freshened up the view from Cassie's bedroom window. She drew back her curtains to see the last grey clouds being chased across a breezy blue sky and the bushes and the trees in the garden glistened in the morning sun. Everything said that this was a new day and Cassie felt a charge surging through her. She checked her mobile for the time: 10.05. Wow! She'd slept right through. She slipped on her dressing gown and stepped out of her bedroom. Downstairs she could hear the voices of Mum and Dad. So, it was true and she hadn't been dreaming; Dad was still here. She made her way into the bathroom for a shower.

It wasn't a morning for a battle over breakfast. Cassie said she would have a bowl of cereal and a cup of tea and her mum didn't press her to have some fruit or toast. She made a fresh pot of tea for herself and Cassie's dad.

"I think I'm approaching tea overload." Dad was trying to break the formal atmosphere which had suddenly dropped about them almost as though they had an evening of excess and now, they must slowly regroup around normality. Cassie looked closely at him as his head was framed by the light of the kitchen window and noticed for the first time how wrinkles were forming around his eyes, bags were developing beneath them and in his temples, there were a significant number of traitorous grey hairs. It was as though this was a dad she had never seen before.

"Dad, why aren't you at work?"

It suddenly dawned on Cassie that the morning was much more unusual than she'd expected.

"I've rescheduled, love, and your Mum's phoned in as well."

It *was* an unusual morning, a unique one of talk and serious deliberations. They sat around the table as Cassie unenthusiastically spooned cereal into her mouth, not tasting the golden goodness which was promised on the packet. There was a lot to discuss but dad did most of the talking.

"Cassie, don't for a minute think that we don't believe you. We do. What possible reason could you have for coming out with such a story in the middle of the summer holidays? We have to have confidence in the police, you know how seriously they took everything last night and I'm sure they will do their best."

Cassie thought back to the earnest face of Kerry. How she'd encouraged Cassie to talk and didn't register any shock or surprise. How many times had she been through that situation? How many stories had she listened to? And how quickly would she pick up on something which didn't ring true?

"I was telling the truth, Dad."

"Of course, you were, Princess."

The word slipped out before dad could stop himself and Cassie grimaced. He carried on, what he had to say was awkward enough without allowing other irritations to intrude.

"But we have to face facts: it might all boil down to your word against his. What real evidence is there? The word of a headteacher against a fourteen-year-old girl?"

A fourteen-year-old girl with an overactive imagination, prone to daydreaming. No-one actually said this out aloud but Cassie thought it to herself and she was sure that they were thinking it too.

"I can see an investigation being carried out," Dad continued, "but it might just end in a reprimand being issued, or a reminder about procedure: don't be alone with a pupil in your office, that sort of thing."

Cassie could see the truth of this but said nothing. This was how it often worked, the great rumbling machine of authority powering over small individuals. This was why daydreams were so seductive; it was where an individual could triumph.

"Which leaves us with a bit of a problem." Dad looked at Cassie seriously. "Neither your Mum nor I want you to go back to that school in September."

Although Cassie wanted to make an immediate objection and she ransacked her mind in double quick time to find reasons why this couldn't happen, it made sense. How could she go back? How could she be one of Mr Brown's helpers? How could she *not* be one of Mr Brown's helpers? A normal school life would be impossible, but what Dad had said was still a bombshell.

"I'd have to leave Ali. She's my best friend."

She looked to her Mum, whose face remained impassive. She'd obviously realised this too but she seemed unmoved and the full complexity was beginning to dawn on Cassie. Not only would she have to leave Alison but they would have to tell her some reason for the change of school. And would Alison be interviewed as part of any investigation? The word would get round all of the parents in the school; rumours would spread. All because Cassie had opened her big mouth and blabbed. Cassie looked at her parents; the shock on her face was too much to hide. She didn't need to say anymore as once again her mum reached out for that comforting hand hold.

"You've done the right thing, love. Never, ever doubt yourself. It's going to be tough for you and you'll find it difficult, but we're here for you, both of us. You've got our support."

Only a few moments earlier that morning Cassie had felt a huge sense of relief; a new charge of life running through her. Now everything was weighing down on her again: the difficulties that were constantly being thrown at her. So, it took a moment or two before Mum's words really sunk in.

"We're here for you."

"Here? What do you mean, here?"

She looked at her dad who was trying, but failing, to suppress a smile.

"Yes, here. I've asked your mum if she will take me back and she said yes. I suppose I really ought to ask you the same question."

"Oh, Dad!"

Cassie kicked back her chair and ran round the table to throw herself around her father's neck.

* * * * *

"If you're going to keep on feeding me spag bols like that, I'll soon be enormous." Cassie's dad placed his knife and fork on his plate. "Delicious," he added, "Terrifico."

"Terrifico?" Is that genuine Italian?"

"Si, si. Bella, bella, bella, terrifico snap."

Cassie laughed again at her father's terrible Italian accent and her mum shared her delight. Dad was back, it was almost like old times. Maybe there would be a silver lining to this horrible grey cloud after all. He was still Dad, of course; still able to make them laugh with his daft jokes, but coming back when he did had seemed to alter him. There was no mention of the fanciful dreams, his fantasies about the future. No, he'd been quite clear and pragmatic in his planning.

"I saw the boss and negotiated a new job description: a desk job in town with only ten minutes travelling time to work. No more long drives, trekking up and down the country on chocablock motorways. And the weekends are ours. Starting this weekend: it's been ages since I've been to the seaside so we'll pack the car and go and have a paddle in the sea. Last one in buys the ice creams."

They all smiled as they took this information on board. There were going to be some big difficulties ahead and some very important decisions to make but they could do it. It was Cassie who spelt it out clearly.

"You've got to mean it, dad. You've got to keep your feet on the ground. It's no good daydreaming."

"Out of the mouths of children, eh?" Dad was still smiling. "No, you're absolutely right; I've done with the daydreams. You can forget this advice."

He'd been toying with the silver snuff box.

"It's been in our family for years this. We'll have to get it valued sometime. It's definitely Victorian silver. I seem to remember someone saying it dates back to the Crimea. Who knows what stories this could tell?"

He closed the lid of the box and pushed it across the Cassie who picked it up and let her fingers run over the fine inscription. Almost inaudibly she wistfully mouthed the words:

"To Will and the land of dreams."

But who was it that lived in the land of dreams? Sure, she had, but wasn't Dad just as bad? Hadn't he been carried away by dreams, didn't he live in a fantasy world? And was it really possible to change so suddenly, to wave a magic wand? The dread feeling suddenly came over Cassie that the warm relief she had felt lately was just a façade, more words without real meaning. But not for her, as far as she was concerned, she was done with Will and his Land of Dreams. Nice boy or not, he was out of her life and she was going to take a much more practical approach; from now on it was feet on the ground time. No more dreams, no more nonsense. Everything now would be done for a purpose.

## Chapter Thirty

# Roots and Reliability

It had been typical of Dad, whenever Cassie showed any enthusiasm for anything, Dad would jump in too. Like the project on Victorian times for instance and the sudden reappearance of the snuff box which may, or may not, have significance for the family. It was usually the case that Dad would wade in and take over.

"It's marvellous what you can find out now," he said. "I've been looking into our family history; there's all kinds of sites you can use now plus parish records, weddings and funerals. We go back hundreds of years, the Jacksons do. What's more, we can be proud of what we've done: coalminers, steelworkers we helped build the country's industrial strength. Good solid workers, us Jacksons."

Cassie had been messing with her mobile trying to block out Dad's pronouncements. Now, quietly fuming, she picked it up again to continue her idle scan of what was happening.

"But here's the really interesting bit," Dad hadn't realised that he was struggling to hold his audience, "We've always been based around these parts. The Jacksons stick around, we're steadfast and loyal. I've traced family members right back to when the Manor Hall estate was run by the Graham family and it was the largest estate in the whole county."

Now Mum, who had been trying to catch up on celebrity gossip in a magazine, finally turned her attention to what her husband was saying. "So what, love? What does all that prove? That we've grafted for other people for generations?"

"No," he was unabashed, "According to this, in the eighteen-hundreds, we had a marital link with the Bells?"

"And who were the Bells when they were at home?"

"At that time, they were estate workers like us."

"So?"

"Except for this one, William Bell who appears in the 1851 census but not in the 1861, no record of him in Parish burials or anything. But think about those dates again and what was happening. The Crimean War of course. I reckon he joined up. I reckon William Bell joined the army. My next step is to check military and regimental records. We've got a hero in the family."

William Bell. Mum thought over the name that ought to register somehow. Where had she heard it before?

"For goodness sake Dad!" Cassie's explosion was as loud as it was unexpected. "Mum's right. What are you getting so excited about? For years we've worked to make other people rich and when we've not done that we've been used as cannon fodder in some country miles away from anywhere. William Bell should have stayed at home. He was a kid; he should have done what he was good at and stayed at home. Putting on a uniform doesn't make you a hero."

The whirlwind moved on as suddenly as it had started. Cassie snatched up her mobile and stomped out of the room leaving behind her bewildered parents. They were so hard to predict, these storms out of nowhere, and so hard to explain. Why had this one been triggered by a reference to a distant family member? What was certain, judging by the slamming of the door and the thumping up the stairs was that these mood swings were becoming more and more violent and as often as not they set up a chain reaction. For either of them now to give an accusatory look or attempt to apportion blame would be to take the first step in a row of their own. Dad was back but it had been far from plain sailing and sometimes, the assignments at work, the projected trips the length of the country began to appeal again.

And upstairs, in her rage, Cassie had flung herself onto her bed and she now glared at the snuff box and its inscription: "To Will and the Land of Dreams." What the hell does he know, she thought, what the hell does he know?

## Chapter Thirty-One

# Everything the Same but Different Now

As the summer faded to its end and the new term began, Simon and Cassie didn't officially go out together. They didn't repeat the cinema expedition and they no longer had school in common. Their meetings were rare and clandestine. Between them they would see little or nothing of each other. Simon had his mates, Cassie, increasingly ploughed her furrow alone feeling her way into a new school, taking note of the groupings and cliques, keeping a wary eye on the teachers who said they were keen for her to settle in. It was a text message brief and to the point which triggered any meetings: Mum was at work and Dad; well Dad was away somewhere. So, Simon would invent an excuse about having to go and check with somebody about something to do with homework and then he'd slink around to Cassie's.

If they did have the pretext of a DVD they rarely paid it any heed. They did drink wine though, there was no shortage of that in the house, and they would glug uncritically from what was available. Nor did they worry about any kind of protocol now, they both knew what they wanted and they had established a routine which didn't require a hesitant procedure or a slow exploration of what would be acceptable. A few words would do:

"So, how are you?"

"I'm fine. And you?"

Then they would lock into an embrace, kissing and beginning the practiced fumble with buttons, zips and hooks and Cassie would rejoice in the power which she now held, reducing Simon into a mumbling plaything. The strong figure who strode around the sixth form area became inarticulate in his desire and need.

"God, you're so beautiful."

Cassie would present him with a list of pop stars, Hollywood actresses and celebrities.

"More beautiful than them?"

"Yes, much more beautiful than all of them."

"Are you just saying that?"

"No."

They kissed, fumbled and petted until the night Cassie broke off the action and said, "Come on."

She stood up from the sofa, stepped carefully around empty wine glasses and took Simon by the hand towards the living room door and then the staircase and then up to her bedroom and he followed without a word.

How sweet he was. How sweet and gentle not wanting to hurt her and how nice it had all been. Nice and rather non-eventful. So that was it, she was one of the girls who had done it and, although she wouldn't go broadcasting this, she was different now, everything was different and yet oddly the same. Over Simon's sleeping body she looked at the cat pictures on the wall. How childish! Footballers posing with their fixed grins and folded arms. How much did she want to emulate them now? Not at all. She would like to stay here with Simon breathing gently beside her for ever.

But it couldn't be for ever. It couldn't even be for the whole night. Simon woke with something of a start and said he had to go. He climbed from the bed and reached for his jeans saying that he didn't fancy being around when Cassie's mum came home from her shift. He pulled his tee-shirt back over his head and then hopped from foot to foot as he fitted his socks and trainers.

"I have to go."

"Simon…"

"Yeah, sure." He walked over to the prone Cassie and kissed her on the forehead. "See you Cass."

He left and there was no further communication between them for days, weeks and then a couple of months. No communication until the day that his mobile buzzed in his pocket and he pulled it out to read Cassie's text:

"We need to talk."

## Chapter Thirty-Two

# Let's Get This Thing Settled

Cassie walked home knowing that the evening that lay before her was going to be one of the most important evenings of her life. That may have been the reason why she was late from school, not so much because she wanted to put the whole thing off, but because she wanted to minimise the amount of time she had to spend in the house before the *let's get this thing settled* meeting. Hence the unnecessary visit to the school library and the research for homework which she already had under control. The buses were quieter at this time after the initial rush of school finishing, even so, she got off the bus two stops early, as in bus stops because she needed time to think: this thing that was coming up, she could do it, she could do it.

Home was difficult, no two ways about it. She'd had to tell Mum first of all and she'd chosen what she thought was the best time when she was on a late shift and there was always that time after the evening meal when the pots had been washed and put away that Mum sat down with a cup of tea to watch some soaps before leaving for work. Increasingly though, Cassie had noticed that it was a glass of wine that Mum nursed in her armchair.

"Mum, should you be doing that before work?"

"This? This is nothing; it just steadies the nerves, that's all."

"Mum, can we talk?"

Mrs Jackson nodded at her daughter sitting on the edge of the big armchair. "You've got the zapper, switch this off."

"Aren't you watching it?"

"No, switch it off."

Cassie picked up the remote and pressed the on/off button. The screen died and Cassie took a deep breath. There was no easy way to say this, but it needed to be said.

"Mum, I'm pregnant."

Mrs Jackson nodded again. As Cassie's words lingered in the quiet of the living room Cassie had no choice but to return the steady gaze which her mum was giving her and the more she looked at her, the more she realised. Her mother had known already, hadn't she? She'd known.

"Oh, Cassie!"

There would be a time soon for asking important questions about the father's identity and dates and plans and maybe even some recrimination, but for now she stood up from her chair and walked across to Cassie and squeezed up next to her and hugged her. Hugged her little girl, the one she had let down so badly, it was a hug for comfort and a hug of recognition of the whole sorry mess which swamped them all.

Dad had to be told as well. If finding the right time with Mum had been difficult, for Dad it was ten times worse and when the words spoken to him finally registered, incomprehension was followed by pain. He didn't shout or bluster, in that moment he just tried to adjust to the new reality of his newly reconstructed life crumbling around him. His Princess was no longer a princess.

As soon as Cassie let herself into the house, she realised that even by the standards of the last few days, something was wrong. There was no noise for a start, no radio playing, no t.v. A big shopping bag and a mess of supermarket carrier bags had been abandoned in the middle of the kitchen floor. Groceries remained unpacked although a stray apple had rolled some distance towards the cooker.

"Mum!"

The downstairs was devoid of life. Cassie started mounting the stairs calling again.

"Mum!"

She found her in her bedroom slumped across the unmade bed. She was fully dressed although she had kicked off her shoes which now lay randomly on the carpet near a pool of solidifying vomit. Inert, she did not respond to the call. Cassie reached her in three quick strides and shook her.

"Mum, are you okay?"

One eye opened in a moment of dull unrecognition.

"Mum, what's wrong?"

But there was the smell, the awful pallor of her mother and the dreadful truth.

"You're drunk!"

The bottle lying on its side told all.

"Vodka!"

"I've overdone it this time."

"Oh God." Cassie looked at the immobile mess lying in front of her.

"We're supposed to be going to the Jones's tonight."

"Where? I've overdone it. Sorry."

Cassie looked around in despair. Where to look for help now? Travelling again, Dad would not be in till late, she knew that. She also knew that everything was down to her now. She brought a damp flannel from the bathroom and cleaned the flecks of vomit from around her mum's face then she took a dressing gown down from a hook behind the door and laid it over the prone body.

"Are you done with being sick? Are you going to be sick again?" There was no answer now. "Oh, bloody hell." Cassie dragged another pillow from across the bed and struggled to insert it under her mother's head. "Let's keep your head higher than your body. I'll fetch a bowl and put it down by the bedside." She was still chuntering to herself as she returned to the kitchen and ransacked the cupboard under the sink. Bleach, she knew, would be a disaster on the carpet but there was a carpet cleaner spray, a rough floor cloth and plenty of kitchen roll. She returned fully armed to the bedroom where she fought and swallowed hard against the sight of the vomit and the smell. She'd given up on her solo commentary now concentrating instead on trying to sort out the mess. She scraped away at the solidifying vomit, picking out unidentifiable lumps from the fibrous texture of the carpet and then sprayed on to the dark patch and looked at her efforts. The damp patch would dry and remain unnoticed, she hoped. The carpet cleaner spray promised *the zingy smell of lemons* and it had done something to alleviate the foul odour but even so Cassie opened the window to let in some fresh air. And a shower, she definitely needed a shower.

"I take it you're not coming tonight?" It was a question asked without any realistic expectation of an answer. Cassie was confirming what had been obvious for some time. "Okay, you sleep it off then." She was on her own now.

Back in the kitchen she popped a slice of bread in the toaster and poured herself a glass of orange juice. She took some low-fat spread from the fridge and a jar of peanut butter from the cupboard. When the bread jumped out of the toaster, she smeared both over her toast and took a bite then she dropped it all into the pedal bin. She could maybe manage the orange juice.

Cassie sucked in her breath as she fastened her jeans and wondered how much longer she would be able to wear them. Thinking which might explain why she pulled out a baggy sweatshirt and pulled it on. It was ridiculous spending time bothering about what to wear for a visit to the Jones's house but she was ready now, as ready as she would ever be.

It was an expressionless Simon who answered the door and showed her into a sombre living room where positions had already been established. Mr Jones sat on the sofa, Simon had claimed a place in an armchair and Mrs Jones presided from a Queen Anne chair. No music was playing, the room was silent; the whole house was silent. Cassie listened for any sound of Ali moving around. There was no sound of Ali. Silence. There was nothing else for it but to go and take a place alongside Mr Jones on the sofa.

"Where's your mother?"

"My mother," Cassie echoed the unfamiliar formal tone of Mrs Jones, "is not well."

"I'd have thought she would be fit enough for a meeting like this."

"She's rung in to work. If she's not going to work, she's not well."

It was Mr Jones who interrupted this early exchange. He stood up from the sofa and stretched.

"I'm sorry, Simon, can I have the armchair? It's much better for my back."

Simon obliged, taking a place next to Cassie on the sofa although he didn't make any eye-contact. How often she'd played and chatted in this room, how often she'd been welcomed as a friend of Alison's with the easy come and go access of friendship. Now Cassie felt the very walls of the sitting room closing in on her and squeezing out her last breaths. It was time to start; Mrs Jones now felt the meeting could get properly underway. There was no offer of any refreshments of any kind as this was strictly business.

"Right, let's get this matter sorted. From what I've been told, there's still time to make the necessary arrangements so that you two don't go messing up your lives completely. What steps have you taken?"

Brisk and efficient, there was no doubt that she was addressing her question to Cassie alone.

"I haven't taken any steps yet. I need time to think, I need time to talk to Simon."

At the mention of his name, Simon lifted his head from his despair and confusion but if he had any words to speak, he would not be allowed to speak them now because his mother moved into full flow. It was only a flimsy barrier which had been holding back the deluge.

"You need time to think! The time for thinking is long past. You should have done your thinking before you… before you took to your bed with my son. Why didn't you think then?"

"Fran." Mr Jones felt he had to intercede.

"Don't you Fran me. This is serious and yet she hasn't even taken any steps yet because she wants to do some *thinking*. She needs to move quickly." She turned her attention back to Cassie. "You need to do something quickly because I'm not going to stand by and watch my son's life be ruined by a little tart."

"Fran! That's enough!"

"Well, that's what she is: a little tart from a feckless family."

Cassie stood up and met Mrs Jones glare full on. She was composed, she knew she had to stay composed and yet inside she shook like a kitten.

"This isn't working. Maybe we can talk later when everyone is a little more calm. But for now, I think I had better go."

"Yes, go. And don't think you'll ever be welcome back here."

"Right! That is quite enough." Mr Jones, bad back or not, was also on his feet now. "Fran this is an emotional moment and everyone understands that, but you've gone too far. You'd better go upstairs and settle yourself down a little." He turned to Cassie. "I'm sorry; you didn't need to hear any of that. Simon, will you walk Cassie home and when you come back, you and I need to have a word."

Trying not to stagger or bump into any of the furniture, Cassie found her way back to the front door. Simon, she realised, was behind her and they both stepped out with relief and breathed in the cool, evening air.

## Chapter Thirty-Three

# She's Got Some Pluck

A cloak of silence was draped around the house when Simon returned. The tension had eased but a residual anxiety, which Mr Jones tried to dissipate, remained.

"I'm making some cocoa. Do you want one?"

Simon didn't think he could drink or eat anything at that moment but he picked up the signs.

"Yes please."

Rather than return to the living room, they sat at a small table in the kitchen cupping warm mugs between their hands.

"Where's Mum?"

"She's upstairs. I don't think she'll be down again tonight."

"She flew off the handle."

"She did. She's upset."

"It didn't really help anything though, did it?"

Matt Jones looked down at the receding level of the cocoa in his mug, staying silent, weighing up the options, not wanting to stray down the path of disloyalty.

"She's been taken by surprise, that's all. It's daughters who are supposed to bring home this sort of news, not sons."

"Ali wouldn't get herself into a mess like this."

"No and neither would you. That's what we thought anyway. *Is* it a mess? Have you thought about what you are going to do?"

It was Simon's turn to pause. Of course, he'd thought about what to do. He'd thought of little else for days now but every avenue he went down turned into a dead end or else it looped around and brought him right back to where he had started from. Some knots are impossible to unfasten. He tried not to be sullen or mutter:

"Mum's not the only one to be taken by surprise. This wasn't exactly planned."

In the cool of the evening a car could be heard being driven too fast for the estate road and nearer to hand the movement of the kitchen clock supplied a regular, rhythmical tick.

"What do *you* think, Dad?"

"I can't tell you what to do."

"I didn't ask you to. I just asked you what you thought."

"Fair enough, for what it's worth, here goes...There was a time when getting a girl into trouble left you with very few options: you could marry her sharpish and let people do the maths for themselves or you could do a runner and be a complete scoundrel."

Even in the seriousness of the conversation this brought a glimmer of light to Simon's eyes.

"I'm not a scoundrel."

"No."

"But there's another option now, isn't there? The one your mother favours. In this day and age women can follow a procedure, tell themselves that they are taking control of their own lives, exercising a right to choose and then carry on as they were."

"A procedure? You mean an abortion?"

"Yes."

"Why didn't you say abortion?"

There was a small kitchen table between them, but little else. This was as close as the father and son had been for years.

"An abortion, yes. I didn't say the word because the very thought of it appals me."

"So?"

"So, nothing. That hasn't got anything to do with me, or your mother for that matter. It's for you and Cassie to sort out."

They had both finished their cocoa. Simon knew that if he collected the mugs now and rinsed them in the sink, he would break this precious thread between his father and himself. He kept his hands cupped around an empty mug and did not move. He was aware of all the stories his mum and dad told, how they met and how they had started off together; the tiny terraced house: *no good for swinging dead cats, I can tell you,* and the early holidays spent under dripping canvas. All of the difficulties which were now recounted as fond jokes.

"Dad… was it easier for you and mum?"

Matt Jones smiled at his son, "The getting together you mean? The setting out on a life together? That isn't ever easy for anyone. But I will say this: that girl came here tonight completely by herself, into the lion's den as it were. She got the worst kind of reception and had her family insulted on top of all that. But she kept her head, kept her dignity. She's got some pluck that girl. Whatever you two decide, you have to respect that, Simon. She's well worthy of your respect and you should make sure that you treat her right."

"You mean…"

"No, I don't mean anything, because respect in itself is not enough. There is a path you could choose, and if you are thinking of going that way then the word love should be right at the centre of your discussions. There, I've said it: love."

Dad didn't usually do a lot of the talking, he'd say it was because he never got the chance, but when he did it was usually to comment on the contents of his newspaper, comments he would air without expecting any kind of response, oblivious perhaps, of Alison and mum swapping smiles which said, *Dad's off on one again*. And now Simon had listened to his father who *hadn't* gone off on one again, he'd brought all of his experience to bear on a pressing issue and left words echoing in Simon's head. It was time for bed now and Simon would go up, but he knew before he even said goodnight that he wouldn't sleep and before he left, his dad left him with one more comment.

"You were some time walking Cassie home, Simon. It's only round the corner to her house, it doesn't take that long, and you came in wet, so I'm guessing you did some talking and I'm thinking that's a good sign. You'll get through this – both of you."

Simon climbed the stairs, visited the bathroom and then went into his bedroom to ready himself for bed.

## Chapter Thirty-Four

# The Darkening Sky

Simon, she realised, was behind her and they both stepped out into the cool evening air.

"Didn't you bring a coat?"

"I'll be fine. It's only around the corner."

He accompanied Cassie step by step with a respectable half a metre between them. He felt he should say something beyond some comment about the cold and imminent rain but what to say exactly was a problem. The silence lengthened, the distance to Cassie's house shortened and it was Cassie, for the first time looking frail and frightened, who broke the silence.

"That wasn't much fun."

"No, I'm sorry. I've never seen Mum like that before. She was…out of order."

"I've never seen your dad like that before either. Wow! Talk about taking control."

"He's alright is Dad."

"What about Ali. Where was she?"

"She was sent on an errand. It was all set up. Narrowing the odds in our favour."

"What has she said about all of this?"

"Nothing."

"Really?"

"Yeah."

It was food for thought. She must have known about everything but Ali hadn't been in touch at all.

They were almost in sight of Cassie's house and the threatened rain was now beginning to fall. Things needed to be said and yet they were just tip-toeing around the big issue.

"I'd ask you in but..."

"But your mum's not well."

"No, she's not."

Simon finally closed the gap between them taking hold of Cassie's elbow and leading her in to the partial shelter of a doorway set in to a garden wall.

"We've been here before."

"Don't remind me. I was a complete idiot running away like that."

"Cassie, there's a lot you aren't telling me, isn't there?"

She couldn't face him. How could she possibly make a start on telling him everything he didn't know? Despite the attempt at sheltering, they were packed together in the doorway now and getting wet. This was all impossible.

"Cassie, that night...when we did it..."

"*When we did it?*" She wanted to laugh at his choice of words.

"When we slept together...I asked you if it was alright and you said yes."

"It was alright."

"But I meant...precautions."

"Did you think I was on the pill or something? Why didn't *you* have anything? Besides, it was our first time."

"You didn't believe that did you?"

No, she didn't believe that, but what could she say? He was sheltering her now in a protective hug. This wasn't a prelude to a kiss or anything else. This was Simon being Simon.

"Simon, that night I wanted to…I wanted to be as close to you as possible, and…you've always been kind to me and you listen to me. It was a special night and you made me feel special. You always make me feel special. Simon… I love you."

Simon looked over the shoulder of this young girl he held in his arms, the girl who was dripping rainwater from her wet hair onto his chest. She was crazy was Cassie, she was also very funny. She was a daydreamer, everyone knew that, but she was also thoughtful and considerate. She was serious and she was a laugh. She was small and frightened and she was brave. Being with her had hi-jacked the vague plans he'd had for the future. Now what had she just said? As if he could have misheard her! He pulled her head gently away from his chest and, as the soft rain whispered around them, he looked straight into the blue eyes which shone even in the evening's gloom.

"I love you too."

They should have kissed. They should have been swept up into a new passion, but this was different, this was recognition of a deep truth; the truth of the darkening sky, the intensifying rain and the crumbling brick doorway under which they attempted to shelter. This was how things were.

* * * * *

As he had known, Simon couldn't sleep. He sat up in bed and rattled off a quick text: *we need 2 talk a whole lot more.*

## Chapter Thirty-Five

# You're an Angel

"Okay, tomorrow it is. A mega walk around the park and we'll slip into the café for a cuppa. My treat…"

They stood together on the pavement outside St John's. Cassie smiled at Stacey, "…and don't forget, ring me on my mobile if you're held up. It won't be a problem; we can be flexible. Until then, wrap up. This wind won't do your colds any good."

"We're both well wrapped and looking forward to tomorrow, aren't we, Bethany?" Stacey leaned into the buggy and chucked her daughter under the chin. "And Cassie; thanks for today, and sorry for making a bit of a fool of myself earlier."

"Hey, we all need a bit of a clear the air from time to time. Don't think about it. I'll see you tomorrow."

"Cassie, you're an angel. See you tomorrow." Stacey wheeled around the buggy and set off for home. There would be a couple of hours of quietness until the schools finished and then the resumption of noise, but then tomorrow she and Bethany were going to see Cassie and Will. And what was it Cassie had said? We won't be stuck like this for ever. Kids grow up and go to school; we'll have to have a serious talk about what we're going to do. She'd talked about catching up on qualifications, brushing up on I.T. skills and making ourselves attractive to employers. That wouldn't be a problem for Cassie, Stacey thought, deliberately misconstruing her comments, with that hair and those eyes, she already looked stunning. There might be a cold wind blowing and there was more grey than blue in the sky, but Stacey made her way home with a skip in her step. It was Cassie, wasn't it? Cassie who had the knack of giving you a bit of zest, of making you feel great.

Cassie hadn't moved from where Stacey had left her. She was fumbling with the cover to Will's buggy which was always difficult to attach properly.

"Need any help with that?"

Cassie stood up to see Alison standing diffidently on the doorstep. She altered her balance as she fastened up her coat aware of the distance which lay between, a much greater distance than a mere two paving stones.

"Yes please. Four hands are better than two. If I pull this cover tight, can you pass the ring over that hook?"

The task which had held back Cassie was soon accomplished and Cassie issued her thanks.

"Can I drive?" Alison was still looking to be helpful and Cassie, who had tried and failed to ignore her all morning, could not refuse.

"We've got quite a journey in front of us. We don't use a bus unless absolutely necessary. Do you need any L plates?"

Alison took charge of the buggy. "You haven't changed at all, have you? Still the funny remarks. No, I don't need L plates, I know my stuff: mirror, indicate, manoeuvre." They set off up the hill. "I've missed you, Cassie… And my nephew is gorgeous."

How much fall-out had settled between them? How much time and effort would be needed to dig through all the rubble that had been dumped in their way? This was totally unrehearsed; Cassie had no idea she would be saying these things.

"A year off before university? Do you know where you're going?"

"Cambridge."

"Jesus!"

"No, Newnham actually."

Alison was right; the funny remarks were still there from both of them: the jokes, the interplay.

"It's the college where Sylvia Plath was a student."

"Sylvia Plath. Poet, right?"

"Bang on. Incredibly intense poems." The admiration shone through in Alison's voice.

"So, let me guess, you're going to read English."

"Right again."

"You haven't changed either, have you?" What are you going to do with an English degree?"

Alison shrugged. "Search me. I'll cross that bridge when I come to it."

Together, they pushed their way up the long gradient, past the run-down shops, past the newsagents with the metal grille reinforced window and past the tattoo parlour where each of them speculated on what would be their ideal tattoo.

"A dragon breathing fire on your bum. That would shake them up at your seminars."

"I've no intention of showing my bum at seminars with or without a dragon breathing fire!"

It wasn't until they reached the Dog and Gun that they stopped for a parting of the ways.

"You know, Ali..." How quickly she had slipped into the old nickname, "...I watched you in the group this morning. You were lovely with all the kids and you mix easily with the mums as well. Do they need people with Cambridge degrees to organise Toddlers' Groups?"

Alison fastened her coat even tighter and faced her friend, the one with whom she had spent so much of her youth and school days; the one who, no matter where she went to study or eventually earn a living, would be the one who was always bound to her through memory and now, of course, family.

"You still don't get it do you Cassie? You always looked to me and built me up, praised me to the skies sometimes, but you always overlooked your own talents and resorted instead to wild fantasies. Do I need to spell this out?"

Cassie nodded dumbly.

"You were the one who was a star in there this morning. You had a special way with all those kids; you were the one chatting easily with all the mums no matter what their background. I spoke to Stacey and she thinks you're an angel."

"Oh, that's just Stacey. She calls everyone an angel."

"Stacey admires you and all your talents. Don't deny those talents Cassie; use them, all of them."

There was a time when Cassie thought her friendship with Alison was a thing of the past, something fatally flawed which had run its course, but she stood on that draughty corner and realised that some things ran deeper than petty jealousies, that competitiveness was fine until it was allowed to get out of hand, that ties of friendship sometimes run deep enough to survive surface damage. There would be a time when they could laugh together again about their exploits at school and on the football pitch. They would be able to recall the plans and schemes they cooked up in each other's bedroom; they might even be able to begin conversations by asking, "Do you remember Miss Jenkins? All that hair falling into her eyes?" Even the wicked impersonations might be taken out of the dusty cupboard and given an airing. They might even begin to make some kind of sense of the evil which had forced a wedge between them. But not now. Now Cassie was a mum and Alison was a gap year student and they had to take stock. They were standing at crossroads braving the gusting wind ready to take their different directions. A steady stream of traffic ploughed up the hill; a few pedestrians stood, loitered only briefly then, ducked quickly into the Mini-market to escape from the noise and bitter gusts of wind, but Alison was right; there were strong ties between them which couldn't, and shouldn't, be allowed to slacken, nor could they be undone by rivalries, whatever their source.

"So, you'll be around until next September then?" Alison nodded in response. "And we'll see you every Monday at Mums and Toddlers?"

Alison nodded again and looked plaintively at Cassie. "I hope you'll see me more than that. I hope you'll invite me round so that I can see this handsome young man and keep an eye on that dope of a brother."

Cassie realised how deep Alison had had to dig to produce those words; they weren't words that could be brushed aside, nor could the sentiment that lay behind them be easily dismissed.

A double decker bus in low gear rumbled past them raising a dust storm from which they both instinctively ducked away but Cassie was too late and some grit lodged in her eye. Alison whipped out a tissue.

"Here, don't rub; you'll only make it worse."

Carefully, she held Cassie's head steady and applied a corner of the pointed tissue. "There! Gotcha! How does that feel?"

Eye streaming, Cassie involuntarily blinked a number of times, but she was fine. The tear running down her cheek was no matter; her friend had done the trick and restored her sight. It was time to move on but Alison's hand still cupped the back of Cassie's head.

"We've been very silly, haven't we?"

"Very silly, both of us."

The hand gently slid to the shoulder and then, in the midst of all the traffic noise and the cutting wind, they wrapped their arms around each other and hugged; hugged as easily and naturally as a flower opening in the sun.

## Chapter Thirty-Six

# Cassandra Jackson Again

*Tart, bitch, slag.* That's not even the half of it. I was called all sorts, sometimes to my face, more often in posts. I'd snared Simon. I used to switch on my mobile knowing that the stuff would be there and I would be pulled towards it, drawn to my daily dose of harm; attention is attention in whatever form it comes. Until I told myself, enough! I'd been there before and I knew all about the craving for being abused. Enough! I closed all of my accounts. Let them demean themselves in their pointless posts.

So, no-one really knows the full story. Mum and Dad do, to an extent, but I think they are just as baffled by life as I am. Dad still can't get his head around why the good things he's always wanted haven't landed in his lap. And even if they did, I don't think he would be satisfied. Onward and upward, he'd say, never content, never happy to settle. What is it that card players say when they realise, they've been dealt the best hand they're likely to get? Stick. Dad never sticks; he always opts to twist even if that means everyone else gets screwed up as well.

Mum's battling though. She came within a whisker of losing her job. She'd had disciplinary measures taken against her, official warnings and all sorts but she says it was me that saved her.

"That was my lowest point, Cassie, my daughter having to clean up my mess while I was out of it. Still, it's good practice for when I'm old and senile."

Cheers Mum. But I still feel guilty about not even realising how big her problem was. Too busy with my own concerns, I suppose.

"I'll never be cured. I'm always in recovery."

Tell me about it, Mum.

The person who probably knows most about my story is Annie Neal. I must stop calling her "the old woman" as she is our friend. Yes, Stacey and I often pop around with the kids and we have a good old chat. Or sometimes she'll say, "I'll look after these two little ones if you two girls could nip down to the shop and get me some tea and a packet of biscuits."

There's always plenty of tea and biscuits in the house but she knows that she's giving me and Stacey twenty minutes on our own. But there was that first meeting in her house when I'd told her everything, absolutely everything, and I couldn't believe what I'd done, unburdening myself like that to a near stranger. But I always remember one of the things she'd said, "You might not know this, but things like that have always gone on. Call themselves grown-ups? Some people never grow up; they never accept the responsibilities of being grown up. And when they're found out, they'll try and blame the kids. Listen, it's never the kid's fault."

No-one had ever said that to me, not Mum or Dad or the police. No charges were ever brought against you know who, I can't even bring myself to say his name, and I've been left to carry around the guilt for ever. *She must have led him on, mustn't she?* And sex, which should be about sharing and caring and love, was more about power. When people look at me now, I can see the darkness in their eyes and I know what's in their minds.

Sometimes, I think I should have stuck around with William Bell. Yes, Private William Bell. He was a gentleman, he would have respected me, put me on a pedestal even and he would be proud to have me as his young lady. But then I stop myself, sometimes I even punch myself as hard as I can on the arm because that kind of rubbish belongs in the past. If William Bell taught me anything it's that there is no such place as the land of dreams. We're here on this earth and we have to make the best of it. There are never any totally happy endings in real life.

All of which brings me back to this flat with all the anonymous banging of doors and shouting from neighbours we never see. Then there's the dismal view. Some people have rose-coloured glasses; I think our windows must be tinted grey: gloomy, dingy grey. And inside I walk the tightrope between happy homemaker and hopeless failure. I always want everything to be nice; I want Simon to be happy – the black shadow that haunts me now is the thought of Simon leaving – and I want to do everything well but then sometimes I just want to throw myself on the sofa and howl at the impossibility of it all.

If there's any way of staying on the tightrope, let alone getting across to somewhere safe, it has to be through routine: the visits to Mums and Toddlers, calling to see Mrs Neale and walking the parks. We still go at weekends; we are in fact world champion buggy walkers and now Will looks like a hiker in the making. He'll shout to get out of the buggy and then toddle along on his chubby legs until he becomes too tired for any more and then Simon will pick him up and carry him on his shoulders. He loves that, they both do.

Do I have dreams for Will? Dreams are dangerous; I know that, so all I hope is that Will grows up to be his own man. But I'd like him to be strong. I'd like him to know that having strength doesn't mean having to fight but it could mean helping others with their burdens, helping those who are less strong. That's a thought, isn't it? If all our kids grew up believing that, what a difference it would make.

We were on our meander through the park last Saturday afternoon heading for the café for our cuppa. I know, we live it up, don't we? Anyway, we were suddenly stopped by a voice,

"Simon!"

I think it was the boots I noticed first, knee-length brown leather boots worn over designer denim jeans and then a snug-fitting patterned sweater. Simon may have noticed something else before the boots. But there was also the blonde hair cut fashionably short. She carried two glossy high street shopping bags.

"Simon, I haven't seen you for ages! How are things?"

"Hello Miss Johnson."

"Oh, Liz please. We don't need any of that Miss stuff now."

"I'm fine. We're all fine. This is Cassie and this is Will."

"Hello. Oh, he's gorgeous. Takes right after his dad."

If she made eye-contact with me at all it was for a nanosecond.

"So, what are you doing?"

"Apprenticeship. Engineering with Hargreaves in town."

"That's very good. But do you know Simon, I always thought you would make a great teacher. Calm, knowledgeable and you could be a great role model for kids."

"No, no, I passed on the university thing."

"Ah but there's loads of ways into teaching now. Finish your apprenticeship and then come into teaching with life experience. Absolutely ideal. Pop in and see me, if I'm still there, that is."

"Why, are you leaving?"

"No, nothing yet. But you don't stay in one place for ever, do you? Onwards and upwards. Listen, I have to dash, but anyway, keep in touch, won't you?"

There was a big smile for Simon, a condescending cooing noise for Will and barely a glance for me and then she was gone, powering her way across the park, swinging her carrier bags as she marched.

"She's nice." I said.

"You hate her."

"How do you know I hate her?"

"Because sometimes I can read you like a book."

The smile I received now was real.

"So, who is she?"

We'd settled in the café and we were looking out over the broad expanse of the park. We must have been celebrating something because to go with our tea we had a piece of brownie, some of which Will was determinedly smearing across his face.

"Miss Johnson, Head of Sixth Form."

"Head of Sixth Form! She only looks to be about twenty-five."

"Going places, isn't she."

It was time to sip my tea and make excuses to fiddle with Will's coat. Simon could have gone places. He made light of it, but he had given up the chance of going to university. I don't know about teaching but I'm sure there were a lot of things he could have gone into. The world beckoned. He could have ended up earning big money and dressing fashionably, looking out for the next big challenge. Instead of that he was spitting on a napkin and wiping chocolate off a toddler's face.

"Simon…" And I could have shot myself even as I began this question. "Simon…what do *you* want to do?"

Knowing Simon, he might have turned my question into a joke. He might have said something like *I'd like to pour more tea* or *I'd like to get home for the football scores.* But he didn't. He could read me like a book and now he'd sensed that this was a serious question, a question about more than the remainder of a Saturday afternoon.

It was sometime before he answered. It was as though he was weighing up all of my anxieties, all of my past which I'd never told him about but which I think he'd made a pretty good guess at, and he was choosing words as carefully as a shopper chooses fruit.

"There's a lot to look forward to. This young man will be going to nursery and then starting school. His mates will be coming round to play, he'll be having birthday parties and if he's not the best footballer for miles around, it won't be his mum's fault. But you know what, that flat isn't the place to be. No matter how hard anyone tries to see it different, it will always be a concrete box in the sky. It's not the place for me, or him, or any of us. So, the question shouldn't be what do *I* want to do, it's a question of what *we* want to do. We need a house with a bit of space, a bit of garden where he can go out and let off steam. We should work towards that, the three of us. What do you think?"

What did I think? It was a bright, breezy day. A bit nippy perhaps but fluffy white clouds were racing each other across the sky, some roller skaters sped through the park and down by the lake a gang of ducks were squabbling over thrown bread crusts. It was a beautiful day, that's what I thought, and there was no reason at all why I should be sitting at a wobbly table, picking up brownie crumbs with the tip of my finger and trying to ignore the tears welling in my eyes.

# THE AUTHOR

Born and brought up in Carlisle, the son of a railwayman, John chose to become a teacher and taught in five schools in all, ending up as an Assistant Head.

He now concentrates upon his own writing and he has been published as poet, short story writer and novelist.

He lives with his wife in Wakefield U.K. where they plot visits to visit their son who lives in Brooklyn, New York.

Printed in Great Britain
by Amazon

41938591R00098